HEATHER S. CHAUVIN

Trouble Inside

For my sister and brothers, who inspired me to write a book about someone who doesn't have any.

Contents

Prologue

If you had asked me this morning what my day would entail, I would have huffed a chuckle and replied with an automatic "Same ol', same ol'." Never in my life did I think I'd discover a dead body. That was not a flicker of a thought. Hell, the idea had never taken up residence in my head at all. I placed it right alongside my nonexistent thoughts of winning the Olympics, running for president, learning to make Spanish paella from scratch (was that even possible?), and becoming the first woman to explore the Andromeda Galaxy. These are all moments I've never thought to imagine, because truly, they never will happen.

Or so I thought. But here I am, frozen and staring at the body lying in front of me.

I'm frozen for many reasons. For one, I've never seen a dead body. Second, I'm not sure he is dead, but his glassy, vacant eyes aren't a good sign. Third, I'm most definitely not supposed to be here. Lastly, I wouldn't know how to resuscitate him even if he seemed to be somewhat alive.

Judging by the amount of blood on the floor, I'm guessing he is not okay. I'm no detective, but I've watched and listened to my fair share of true crime documentaries, and this looks like one of those crime scene photos they show or recreate. That's not good. This will be a crime scene photo. The only reason it isn't yet is because I'm still just standing here, hardly breathing.

Ugh.

I shouldn't be here.

God, I really am not supposed to be here, and because I'm not supposed to be here, I can't call 911—not that urgent assistance would help this poor guy.

I inhale sharply to clear my mind, and I try not to blow out too much air, worried my spit may escape with my exhalation. That would be a problem.

I need to make a decision immediately; otherwise, it will be made for me. I can call 911 and report the body anonymously, but then they'll suspect that I'm the killer and try very hard to find me despite my anonymous call. Not going that route.

I can report it and tell them who I am, but then they'll get me on alternate charges, and they may still suspect me of murder. Scratch that option off.

I can go now and leave without saying anything before anyone sees me or I leave behind evidence I was here.

That could work. That way, the police don't worry about finding me, and they find the actual killer—if this was a murder and not just some crazy accident. The third option, the choice to leave, seems to be my best one. The only thing is that I'll have to live with this secret. I can't tell the police who I think did this. I can't tell them anything that I saw before I walked in, which means I may have to face the fact that a killer may escape without prosecution. Just to save myself? Am I that selfish?

I take one more look, committing the scene to memory, before I carefully step backward out of the house the same way that I came in.

Chapter 1

BEFORE THE MURDER

Every day is the same, mostly. My blaring alarm jolts me awake at four a.m., and I proceed to set it to snooze, scrambling each time to press the button in the hope of returning to the dream world. And the whole process repeats until I decide I should probably begin to compose myself for work. The problem is that I know I can leave the house at 4:55 AM and likely show up to work exactly on time, if not a little late because of unforeseen traffic.

What's the point of waking up that early, anyway? That's what I ask myself every morning. It's not like I wear makeup, although I could use a little of it to cover some dark spots. I don't eat breakfast because I'm never hungry until after twelve. I don't go to the gym, but that's really because I already wake up early enough for work. Fortunately, living so close to work means that I can never really be all that late. If I were late, well, I wouldn't just get in trouble with my boss but also with all the people who are expecting my deliveries so that they themselves can start their day.

I finally pull myself from my comfortable silk sheets, and I can almost hear them whispering for me to return. Although that's surely simply my own desires filtering through my head. I walk groggily to my attached bathroom and turn on the lights to break the fog. I stare at my squinting eyes in the mirror and take in my appearance. My curly blond hair lies in knots and tangles atop my head, which are likely a result of my tossing and turning all night. I open my brown eyes wider to ensure they're not bloodshot, and although they are not, bags still lie under them. Luckily, I see no new pimples today, just the same large red one that's been wreaking havoc on my right temple for a few days now. I proceed quickly with my morning routine: brushing my teeth and hair, cleaning and moisturizing my face, and then done!

I scurry back into my room and throw on my work outfit — jeans, a company-branded navy blue polo shirt, socks, and worn black high-top sneakers. Now I'm truly ready, the fog of sleep fading to my periphery.

As I walk out the door, I chuckle to myself, thinking, *At least I don't need to make coffee.*

I'd honestly walk to the shop, since it's so close to my house, if it weren't for my need to drive my car to do my job. I live in a small town called Houma, nestled in the bayou state of Louisiana, although I feel like it gets bigger and more crowded every year. This early in the morning, hardly anyone is out on the roads, and it only takes me a total of one left turn and one right turn to get to Coffee Beams. Yes, Beams, not beans like one would think. That's because our logo brand revolves around the sun, just like everything does, technically. We provide bottled iced coffees for all the coffee lovers out there who start the day as soon as the sunbeams hit the pavement, if not earlier.

Although my drive to work may be short, I spend the entire

shift driving from one stop to another, delivering iced coffees to the lucky individuals who can get their orders placed before our inventory runs out.

For the most part, my schedule is consistent, since most of our patrons are regulars with repeat orders. Some people change the flavor up here and there, modify the usual quantity, and move the delivery date. Very rarely does a business or individual back out of their established delivery. We also get lots of individuals and companies who want to try us out to see if we are a good fit.

I say "we" a lot because I feel like a valued member of the team here. My boss, Kristi, includes me in a lot of decisions and doesn't tell me what to do, instead asking my opinion before determining how she'll proceed with daily operations. She doesn't have to do that. I appreciate her so much for offering me the chance and not necessarily making me feel like it's an obligation I am to fulfill. I'm lucky to love my job, because I hear about many people who can't say the same.

The waking-up part is really the only job requirement that gets to me. Good thing I serve coffee for a living. As I reach the front counter, Kristi smiles at me and slides my coffee across it.

"Hey, Zoey! Ready to deliver some sunshine?" she asks me.

I chuckle and roll my eyes, because this is the first thing she says to me every day. Her question is like clockwork.

I give one of my typical responses: "Sunshine is my middle name!"

It's a cute little thing that we do. Her prompt is always the same; meanwhile, I rotate among a few responses, and she loves to guess which one I'll use.

"Dang. I for sure thought you'd say, 'But I'm already here'

today."

I smirk at her and tilt my head.

"Hmm, my turn to guess," I say as I stare intently at my bottled iced coffee, which is already beginning to shine with perspiration. "White chocolate mocha?" I purse my lips while asking.

"Now, how did you guess that right?" she asks me, tilting her head down and looking up around her small square-framed glasses to make direct eye contact with me.

"*Mais, cher*, it's a talent that I possess. I'm not a *couyon*," I say, imitating my best Cajun accent in an attempt to make fun of her consistent use of the word.

We giggle together, and it's nice because we don't have to force pleasantries and small talk between us. Although she's my boss, she's also become one of my best friends after we've worked so closely together these past five years. For instance, I know that the current straightness of her black hair is natural, an attribute I would have loved to have had as a teenager. Over time, I've learned that she loves to mix Cajun French terms into her speech, while I, although exposed to them my whole life, still can't say them right. I also know that she considers her light brown eyes too widely set, and they may be slightly, but it could be far worse. She doesn't care about her weight and enjoys our Southern delicacies without shame. It's not like she is an unhealthy person, but living down here, it's impossible not to eat fried food at least three times a week.

I, too, adore all the jambalaya, etouffee, and fried soft-shell crabs. I try to eat the things that bring me joy in moderation, but it's probably these delicious coffees that really do me in. We may not be skinny, but we're also not morbidly obese.

"Well, I have all your orders ready," she says. "Want me to

help you load up? We can save the chitchat and catching up for later."

"Yes, ma'am, that's fine by me."

"You do realize that you don't have to call me ma'am, *vielle*? I'm only three years older than you."

"Yes, I do, but you're the boss, and my momma raised me with manners."

"Yeah, yeah. So you say."

Kristi helps me load a dozen orders into the back of my blue SUV. I have quite a few boxes in there so they can be mostly organized by location and avoid spilling in transit. I'll have to come back to pick up more throughout the day, though, since the coffees have to stay refrigerated here and I can't have them all sitting in my car, getting warm. Well, I mean, I could, but that would be bad for business.

"Thank you for your help, *ma'am*," I tell her as she loads the last couple of orders into my vehicle. I press the button that lowers the hatch and then rest my hands on my hips.

She rolls her eyes at me.

"Have fun! What ya listening to today? Have you decided?"

I tap my chin with my index finger and look up to the side.

"Maybe some elder emo music. I'm feeling dark today," I say with a laugh, because she knows I'm the furthest thing from dark but love some semi-hardcore music now and then.

"Finished with that creepy podcast series you were listening to?"

"Yes! Just finished it on the way home yesterday. It was so good that I just sat in the driveway until the last episode was over."

"All right, then. Be safe on the road! I'll see you soon with the next batch," she says as she walks backward to the glass doors of the coffee shop.

I give her a small wave as I open the driver's-side door with my other hand.

"See ya later."

As I drive away to make the first deliveries of the day, I wonder what she'd think if she knew my secret.

Chapter 2

The first batch of orders for the day usually consists of single beverages or bulk business quantities. As the day goes by, I deliver bulk orders only to people who want to stock their fridges for the week, or a company that needs an evening pick-me-up to get them through the rest of the day.

First thing in the morning like this, people want their coffee! Such a crazy time to see people — very early, before they get their caffeine fixes. I say crazy because when I see my customers out and about organically around town later in the day, they look much livelier and more put together.

I like being that person for them. The person who can deliver a product that turns their whole day around. I enjoy being a light for them. Maybe I'm overthinking it, because in the grand scheme of things, I'm not doing much for them. I mean, they pay and I deliver a product. It really is that simple. But I like to think I do more. I have to feel like what I do matters to those around me. I like to tell myself that perhaps they couldn't do what they do if it weren't for me getting them their coffee without hassle.

Whether I'm delivering to a stay-at-home mom who needs the energy to muscle through a day of solo parenting, a father waiting at the hospital for his child to recover from surgery, or a teacher who looks forward to getting their coffee as one of the best parts of their day, I like that I can do that for them. Literally provide them with the energy to accomplish their goals.

Kristi's business runs like a well-oiled machine, but she has a lot of responsibilities. While she runs the business overall and enjoys making the coffee, one of my neighbors, Quinn, organizes the deliveries for me through our business app. Our establishment is a small business. We have two other girls who help make the coffees, and I'm the one who delivers them. Typically, one of the other girls steps in to help deliver if I'm ever sick or on vacation. Quinn is a godsend. She sits back at the shop and updates the orders as they come in, organizing them in the best order for me to deliver. So although my route is typically the same, it occasionally widens and changes for me to scout additional areas so that I may proceed with my guilty habit.

Even better, Quinn uploads all the addresses sequentially, and our sales system connects to GPS, so as I complete my deliveries, I can mark them in the system, which will direct me to the next location. I'm happy the app doesn't keep track of my route or travel time, since I often like to detour, whether to stop at the store, chat with a friend, or participate in other more unsettling activities that my boss would look down upon my doing while I'm on the clock.

Actually, for all I know, maybe the system that we use for deliveries does indeed monitor my geographical location and drive time. Kristi has never mentioned it, and neither have I, for fear that she may learn the truth or that asking those questions may cast suspicion upon my criminal activities. After all, why drop any hints for her when she appears so clueless about my illicit behaviors? It's better not to draw attention to it.

Instead, I just tell myself that the software does the bare minimum for me to perform my menial duties. I'll likely never find out unless the authorities catch me and prosecute me. The police could subpoena the information to determine my innocence or guilt. Only then will I truly know if my boss knows where I am at all times and how long I linger on the clock in between deliveries. I think that I will already have been condemned by then. So let's hope that never happens.

I think that's why I enjoy breaking the law in the way I do. The thrill of the idea of being caught entices me as much as it fills me with anxiety. I must suffer from some sort of mental complex.

My phone dings then, causing me to glance down and see the alert indicating that my first drop-off location is nearby. I don't need the reminder, since the local gym is a usual order. I did need a reminder to refocus my thoughts, though. I walk in, smile and wave, drop off their iced coffees, and walk out the door—no signature or verification required. We have never had a problem before, since I deliver all my orders as expected. I may not be the most innocent person, but I do my job right.

The rest of the morning goes by like this. Drive, stop, deliver, leave. My phone alerts me to all stops and quantities of coffee to deliver.

Soon it's time for me to return for the next batch of coffees. Even that's programmed in the app, as if the notification is needed. I can't deliver coffee if there is none left in my vehicle.

When I pull back up to the shop, the shop door opens before I even fully put the vehicle in park.

I rush out to greet Kristi and prop the glass door open as she starts heading to my car to begin loading up the next round. Before the car has fully warmed back up to match the damp heat outside, I jump back into the vehicle and switch the ignition on to blast cold air instantly.

I open the app on my phone and begin my route. These first two shifts usually drag on, because, as you can imagine, most people want their coffee first thing in the morning. I live for my fourth and fifth deliveries of the day. Usually, those individuals aren't in a rush, just stocking their fridges. Then afterward, I somewhat dread the last round of deliveries, since once again it feels like crunch time to deliver to those who are expecting their afternoon pick-me-ups.

The next two rounds of my day feel sluggish. They come before the high point of my day, which is the period after my morning work and before my lunch. I put on some music to hold me over until I can begin to scout my next victim. For now, I can sing along to the melancholy melodies. Music is my go-to source of entertainment. I usually choose to listen to music because sometimes I get so focused on observing the houses on my route that if I listen to an audiobook or podcast, I zone out and don't recall what was said.

I typically study my route as if I'm preparing for a test that will determine my future, though not in the ways in which one might think. No, in my case, I detail every home, the presence or absence of cars in the driveway, the presence of maids or laborers, the maintained and manicured lawns that indicate the employ of a lawn care worker, anything to identify possible habitation by children or teens, and most importantly, the presence or absence of doorbell or exterior home cameras.

For weeks, I committed all these details to memory in an attempt to identify a house with a consistent daily routine that is never broken. I don't often choose the nice houses that have two stories, pressure-washed driveways, or attached garages, or the buildings in pristine, well-maintained condition; they may contain hidden surprises. A wealthy businessman able to work from home, or a stay-at-home mother whose husband's wealth allows her the luxury to remain home in comfort. Not to mention that those types of homes are also often more inclined to be equipped with exterior cameras to ensure the residences remain safe and protected.

I am nosy at my core. I enjoy watching individuals, how they reside in their homes, and how they interact with others in their community. I get so much satisfaction from watching and dreaming up situations that I believe these people may be experiencing. I find pleasure in pretending to know the conversations that those that I see out and about are conducting.

For example, as I sit at this stop sign and look both ways—as one should when they come to a stop at a stop sign—I see a blond woman walking her dog on a leash. As she goes, she ends up passing a gentleman walking in the opposite direction. I quickly take in the scene: the body language and facial expressions. Which means that I also see the moment that the gentleman motions for the young lady to remove her headphones.

As I drive away, I play out the rest of the scenario, which I'm not privy to, as though I am still there and watching those two from the shadows. I set the scene in my head: the young woman in her athletic shorts and tennis shoes, poised with one hand on her hip and the other holding the dog's leash. She's too nice. Doesn't want to ignore the man but doesn't feel comfortable stopping to speak to him. I imagine that her watch is counting her walk as an exercise and it'll stop automatically if she also stops. Her irritation is notable in her voice as she asks the man what he wants—politely, of course.

He apologizes for disturbing her, but he has seen her around and is curious to determine where he knows her from. But that's just his pickup line. He's been watching her and memorizing her routine, coming up with the perfect approach. But this attempt, the one he's been planning and scheming over for weeks, fails. She affords him a weak smile and states simply that she walks this path every Tuesday and Thursday and that's probably why she looks familiar. Before he can make another attempt to impress her or appeal to her, she cuts him off, wishing him a nice day and explaining that she has to go, before quickly reinstalling her earpiece so that if he responds, she can pretend not to hear him.

Sometimes, I'll stop there, the imaginary situation complete as I continue memorizing important details from my route. Other times, I spiral. For example, I begin to think about how the young man is hurt by the brush-off. He's disappointed that he was unable to charm the young lady. Without thinking, he chases after her, so overcome with rejection and hurt that he can't think straight. He grabs her from behind, placing his hands over her mouth. The young lady drops the leash, and her dog, a Pomeranian, sits there surprised and unbothered, watching as the man pulls its owner into the shadows.

My imagined scenarios are never consistent. Sometimes they escalate frightfully, and others end joyfully. They are brief and usually fleeting, these daydreams of mine. I have a superior opportunity to be as nosy as one can be. I can watch everyone, and they may be none the wiser. I often push my imagination to the side to focus instead on the primary objective at hand. Most of the time, I'd rather choose to focus on identifying my next victim. I'd rather prioritize finding the perfect home: one with little foot traffic, no cameras, and no homeowner present.

I'm lucky that my job affords me the opportunity to scout the perfect home to invade without arousing suspicion from neighbors. By all accounts, I blend in with the daily traffic of mail carriers, delivery drivers, and individuals who actually belong. I cruise the streets, always following the speed limit and adhering to stop signs so as never to draw any unnecessary attention to my car. Our company logo is displayed on a magnet on each side of my vehicle, so even if anyone does begin to suspect me of ill will, their accusations will soon fall by the wayside. Irrelevant, since I am just a lowly coffee-delivery woman going about my daily delivery route. Nothing more and nothing less. Or so they think.

Chapter 3

I always feel a plethora of emotions in the hours leading up to entering a target's home. As the day begins, I merely look forward to the break-in, trying not to get my hopes up just in case anything happens to postpone or halt the process. The morning is usually a battlefield of feelings: excitement, trepidation, exhilaration, and anxiety competing for victory. As the hour approaches, I'm always filled with jitters, since my emotions induce tangible symptoms that saturate my every move and breath.

Despite my quirky hobby, I typically like to consider myself an average young woman. For instance, I occasionally wear athletic clothing, but I don't prioritize or even consider exercising. I enjoy listening to music from multiple genres. I drink socially. I don't smoke. Unlike some women my age, I'm reluctant to follow current trends and prefer my tried-and-true wardrobe and accessories. Occasionally I succumb to the bandwagon as far as shoes are concerned, but I love shoes, so that's to be expected. I love to consume caffeine in various forms. Childhood trauma? Yeah, sure, doesn't everyone have a little bit of that?

Actually, as a young child, I required counseling for some behavioral issues. To put it mildly, my mom couldn't handle me. I was a terror, throwing fits throughout my childhood, unfazed by reprimands. And as far as everyone knows, I've been able to overcome those anger issues. I no longer lash out by breaking walls and punching people unprovoked. Truly, I don't act like that anymore. Everyone believes that I just grew out of it, but what many people have failed to realize is that instead I now channel my emotions in a different manner than I did before.

I haven't been to therapy recently, so I could be totally off base with this assumption, but I think the reason that I do what I do is that it's an outlet for me. Some people may develop obsessive and compulsive habits, while others may simply twirl their hair, drink too much, bite their nails, or find comfort in drugs. I feel like I have a different coping mechanism. Not to say it's any less dangerous to me or others. It really could be dangerous. I don't technically cause anybody harm, and my intentions are never evil or maniacal. I do what I do because it makes me feel good; it makes me feel better.

As long as I can remember, I have always been a curious person and unable to help myself. When I hear someone gossiping or whispering, I'll often prance into the room and demand that they tell me what they were discussing. I say I demand that, but I read the room first. Some people respond better if I'm less direct. They have that saying, of course—"You can catch more flies with honey than with vinegar."

I like to know the ins and outs of things, even if they're about people I don't know directly. And it's for no reason at all. I don't gossip or share the things I learn; I just enjoy the ability to know things that others are not privy to. I am a seductress of secrets, if you will.

I'm not sure if there's a name for my compulsion, the one

that leads me to perform devious acts that violate the privacy of those I choose at random. I haven't looked it up for fear of leaving a trace or indication to someone about my bad habit. I'm not even sure if it's classified as a compulsion, since I don't see a therapist and have no formal diagnosis. I've never received professional advice on the matter at all, in fact. I don't know what it is, whether it's normal, or whether it has a name. I do know that what it drives me to do isn't legal.

I find great pleasure in entering strangers' homes and digging through all their things. I mean, what would I even look up in a search engine to see what my disorder is? "House hunter"? "Home invader"? "Nosy Nancy"? "Looky-loo"? I feel like none of those names quite defines my unique habit. I live for the joy of knowing other's secrets, just as much as I do for the thrill of getting caught, or evading capture. I find enjoyment in knowing about an individual's secret possessions and the condition of their home when they're not expecting visitors.

One of my favorite things to do is to leave a few items different from how I find them, letting me often speculate if people notice or not. That's one part of the process I wish I could gain more insight into. I may never learn the truth. I refuse to enter the homes of those I know, so I forfeit the chance to learn the answer.

I know that what I do isn't normal, and I can't explain why I continue to do it. I can almost equate it to the experience of riding a roller coaster. Sure, it can be dangerous, but it doesn't have to be. Roller coasters are scary, but people enjoy being scared!

Truly, the only downside to my preferred extracurricular activity is that it's illegal to enter strangers' homes. It's not like I ever do anything nefarious. I have no ill intent, and I never intentionally cause harm or destruction of property. I'm just dreadfully nosy, and I always have been. I've basically found a way to cure it, for the most part. To anyone else, I seem like your typical nosy person. In reality, I'm almost akin to the crazy ones who watch their neighbors out of the windows, keeping a detailed log of cars that enter the neighborhood. Instead of being obvious about it, I hide it.

My friends and family know I'm nosy, but they think it's a little quirk I have. They don't realize how serious it is. They don't understand that I'm technically far more curious than most.

I don't know the exact reason for my unorthodox quirk. I know it's probably something I do to appease a part of me, like because of a deep-rooted psychological motivation.

Thanks to social media, I've learned over the years that many people have experienced some level of trauma, even if they don't realize it. People's trauma manifests in lots of ways that don't even occur to most of us.

I've heard of individuals who wet the bed, or become people pleasers, but I've never experienced anything like that. I'm not so self-centered to think that I'm any different. I just can't see the connection, or identify a solid inciting event. I did have a night terror once and some insomnia here and there, but those stopped around the same time my erratic behavioral outbursts did, as a young child.

I actually looked it up once: *trauma in relation to extreme curiosity.*

Even after I read through a few of the results, none of the triggers struck a chord for me. I saw terms like *abuse, neglect, lack of trust.* At that moment, I couldn't say I had an epiphany or realization. I didn't have a normal childhood, but I didn't have a disastrous one either.

So then I go to thinking maybe I have repressed trauma, possibly from a situation that I believe I could have avoided with more information. Maybe I simply find comfort in knowing that other people are just like me? Maybe I'm lonely and I like to find validation in discovering that I'm not actually as alone as I feel about my hobbies and habits? Who knows? For now, I have a routine that feeds my addiction, and it makes me happy. That'll have to suffice.

I'm sure one day I'll meet someone, have a kid, and become so busy that, surely, I'll have to stop. Until then, I'll continue what I do and wait for the day that I can finally quit my bad habit and instead only reminisce. Even then, I'll never forget the unique, fun, and even ostentatious belongings that people hide away in their homes. I'll always recollect my discoveries fondly.

No one would believe the kinds of things I find in people's homes. That's the best part. I know, and so do the owners, but it's likely no one else does or ever will discover some of what I find. It's thrilling to know someone's secrets, and it's even more riveting because they don't know that I know.

For example, in one home with crosses and Bible verses adorning the walls, I discovered a hidden journal documenting lewd extramarital affairs. One home was clean and tidy as could be, until you entered the master bedroom, which was a hoarder's paradise. In another home, I found a room that contained toys for the kids and a separate locked room that held toys for the parents. Well, it was locked until I found the key. See? These are cherished secrets that not many know. But I do! I'm sure even more outrageous things await me in the expensive and elaborate homes, but I can't get into those without getting caught. At least not yet.

After an uneventful and typical morning, it's finally time! Easily the most anticipated event of the month. It's time to go house hunting. *No, I don't like that one.* Domicile digging? Meh, I'll come up with something one day.

As I near the house, I drive by slowly, performing one final canvass of the area to make sure no cameras have been installed, no one is home who shouldn't be, and that no neighbors or joggers are nearby, since they may pass while I attempt to break in. I make my way toward the back of the neighborhood and turn in to the empty driveway of an unoccupied house that's currently for sale, further concealing my presence here by ensuring that no one identifies my vehicle.

As I approach my target, I press the brakes slowly and steer my vehicle to the right side of the road, the same side as the house. I look around and don't see anyone. Perfect. I double-check that my hair is still tightly wound in a low bun, and I also pat my pockets to ensure that my latex gloves are there. I ease myself slowly out of my car and walk confidently toward the side of the house where the side-entry door stands. The key is to act like you belong so as not to attract attention or alert any passersby. As I approach the door, I shake the nerves from my system. I just can't help it. The excitement, the anticipation, and the fear all mix and send repeated shocking jolts to my nervous system.

As I round the corner of the house to find the side door, I slip on the blue gloves—an almost unnecessary precaution but an implemented step in my process nonetheless. I turn the knob on the off chance that it is unlocked, because I occasionally find that homes in the area are indeed left open throughout the day, whether from forgetfulness or the small-town ambiance of safety, there's no telling. Today's my lucky day, since the knob turns easily, and, with just a slight push, the door swings inward. I pause a moment to ensure no one inside has detected me and to ensure there's no animal that I didn't realize the homeowner had.

When I hear nothing, I take one more look around to make sure that I'm still alone outside, with no witnesses in sight, and I step over the threshold and into the safety of a stranger's home.

Chapter 4

I close the door behind me lightly and take a deep breath to center myself. As I inhale, the subtle scent of vanilla wafts by. The hardest part is over. The house is now my playground in which to do as I please. I can go wherever I want and start in any room that I wish to explore. In general, I try not to stay too long, just an hour or so. Although I know no one is supposed to be home, I also know that things happen that are out of my control. The homeowner could get sick and come home. Maybe they forgot their lunch and turned around to get it, or maybe they had a medical checkup and got to leave the office early. Yes, two hours at most to be safe, and even less time if my jitters get the best of me.

I have no idea what the layout of the house is, but that doesn't matter. I'll see it all in due time. Looking around the room, I see a washing machine, a dryer, laundry baskets overflowing with clothes, and towels thrown about the room haphazardly.

I don't think I need to spend much time digging in this room; I can't imagine there's anything the occupants would keep in here. I traverse the speckled white tiles slowly, my footfalls echoing lightly as I go, reverberating off the walls of an empty, quiet house. The laundry room door is left ajar, allowing me to see into the rest of the building. I'm looking directly into the living room. To the right is the front of the house, where a foyer to the front door rests directly beyond the living room.

On the left is a counter, which divides the living room from what appears to be a spacious and outdated kitchen. Brown wooden cabinets and black marbled Formica countertops cover the area. Straight ahead, a large dining room expands the width of both the kitchen and living room. After the dining room, there seems to be a hallway, which no doubt leads to the bedrooms and bathrooms.

I decide right there to investigate the master bedroom first. I don't have a plan, and I never do. I just do what feels right when I enter a home. The weeklong delay before I could enter this house has me fiending to discover something juicy and interesting. Most people hide what they don't want seen in their bedrooms.

But first, I must determine what sign I'll leave behind this time to indicate my infiltration into this home. As I look around, I see a very lonely and unusual black cat figurine resting on a side table in the living room. I lift the object, its weight causing my hand to dip underneath the seemingly light decoration. As I walk toward the kitchen, I analyze the small but heavy sculpture and realize the cat's standing erect on a book. I think the object is a bookend, but I haven't seen the other one. As I rest the figurine gently on the empty counter in the kitchen, I smile to myself, knowing the tinge of confusion that will creep into the homeowner's subconscious upon discovering the item's new location.

I turn around and head toward the hallway, where my foot glides over the threshold; the speckled tile transitions, and my shoe lands on glistening hardwood floors. The aroma of vanilla is less prominent here, as now I smell more of a musky scent.

It's not strong, but it lingers. The smell may be normal for this house and just stand out more because the scent is unfamiliar to me.

I walk eagerly through the hallway, slowing only as I reach the first door. All of them are open, which means that I'll save time, and it lessens my anxiety because I can see into each room and determine if it's empty and what kind of room it is. The first door leads to a bathroom. Next appears to be an office, and the one after that is a spare bedroom. That leaves one more room at the end of the hallway, which must be the large master bedroom, since it's dead center in the hall, meaning the space occupies both sides of the house. I cross the threshold into the large room and find high tan carpeting.

A bathroom door sits across the room to my left, and on the opposite wall lies a closet. The king-size bed rests in the center of the room. I get to work rifling through dressers, digging delicately and ensuring I leave everything as it is. I generally try to leave everything undisturbed. Almost everything, that is.

I've already completed my favorite part of the whole process, which is blatantly leaving one thing awry somewhere in the house. I usually take my time choosing which item I leave out of place or askew. This time, I can't help myself after having prolonged the scouting process.

The last time I entered a home, I pulled the toilet paper down from the horizontal wall dispenser so that four perforated sheets were hanging instead of just one. Subtle, right? In the house before that, I moved the salt and pepper shakers on the dining room table from one inch to five inches apart.

I find an additional thrill in leaving just a small hint that the home has been disturbed. It always bothers me slightly that I don't ever get to see the residents' reaction. The "not knowing" is unfortunate. Not knowing if they spotted my insidious alteration to their home. Not knowing whether they noticed my presence at all. Not knowing if they become scared and question their findings.

I wish I could see if they notice and how they rationalize what they find. Do they get scared? Blow it off? Blame someone else? Begin to lock their doors and watch their backs more often? I wish I could know that. I often scroll through social media and neighborhood forums, but so far, I've never seen anybody share anything.

I zone out of reality and into a world of delight as I lose myself in exploration. Erratically, I scurry about, finding hidden gems throughout the master bedroom—a tattered childhood blanket that's seen better days, laxatives, cosplay fare (wings and crowns for some reason), and a shoebox marked Taxes that houses a half-empty bottle of liquor.

I work my way from the bedroom and back toward the laundry room, one room at a time. I'm almost ready to call it a day, having replaced everything in its original home—except for the bookend, of course.

I've searched all the rooms in the hall, and today I'll skip the living room and kitchen, since they're likely more traveled areas that appear to be in pristine condition.

That's when a very distinct copper odor enters my nostrils. I freeze where I am, looking around the living room to try to identify the source of the smell. Everything appears as it was before, nothing disturbed and no doors or windows open; blue throw pillows rest on a tan sectional sofa, which frames the boundary of the room. The rug in the middle and the hardwood floor surrounding it seem to be clean. I spin around slowly, eyes moving vehemently, in search of the source of the scent.

My gaze stops as it settles upon a small red puddle. I can just barely see it as I look over the counter that separates the living room from the kitchen. My thoughts begin to bounce around in my head. I can't help but imagine scenarios, both chaotic and rational, to explain the small suspicious mess that may be blood. Or possibly just ketchup. But why would ketchup be on the floor of an otherwise clean house? Maybe the homeowner was in a rush this morning and had to leave the mess for later. But who eats ketchup for breakfast? And why do I smell that tangy copper scent? Perhaps the homeowner cut themselves this morning and went to the hospital instead of work. If so, they may be back sooner rather than later. Regardless, I must investigate further to assuage my speculative brain.

I slowly walk toward the edge of the counter in an attempt to learn more about the mysterious puddle. To my dismay, the odor grows stronger upon my approach. As I walk closer, I can see more and more of the kitchen over the counter—the stove, the small bronze handles on the lower cabinets, the white-tiled floor, and a larger puddle of blood. I freeze. It's definitely blood, and it looks like this injury wouldn't have sent someone to the hospital but to the morgue. When did this happen? Has the blood been here the whole time? Where are the police, the sirens, the homeowner?

I push out a breath, afraid to move farther, but I have to try to understand what's happening so that I know what to do next. I tiptoe forward, my eyes searching the pool of blood for a weapon, a body, or, ideally, a fake blood bag spewing the dark liquid. Anything to help me understand, but as I crane my chin up and see more of the floor, my eyes find the unconscious body of a man lying face up in the pool of blood. I say unconscious, but the hazy stare of his open eyes indicates that he's more than unconscious. This man is dead.

Chapter 5

I got out of there so fast. I didn't know what to do. As hard as it was, I blocked out the sight, and I finished my deliveries for the day. Kristi could tell that I wasn't myself, and when she asked me about it, I told her that I didn't feel well. That wasn't a lie. I don't feel well. I'm just not physically sick. Rather, I feel mentally sick. She left me alone for the most part, with no chatting or questions. Instead, she told me to head home and rest, as well as to text her if I still didn't feel well tomorrow.

Tomorrow. Something that man in the kitchen won't get to see. All I've done since getting home is replay my decision mentally. When I try to do anything else, my thoughts drift inadvertently back to that moment. To that man. I don't even know his name, for goodness' sake. I sat down on the couch shortly after I got home and didn't move after that. The TV remains off. My phone stays untouched. But my thoughts—my thoughts rage and crash uncontrollably through my head. Just when I think I'll get up to do something: eat, drink, do laundry, or pee, another monstrous wave of rumination pulls me under it.

I should drink something. *What was the last thing he drank?*

I need to eat. *What was his favorite food?*

I'm tired. *He'll never wake up.*

I just left. I didn't call for help. I simply ran away.

I try to reason with myself too. I didn't do anything to him, and I couldn't save him. At least I don't think I could have. I still feel so guilty. I keep coming up with more questions. It's cruel not to know the answers.

When was he killed? I'm no medical examiner, I haven't touched him, and I've never seen a dead body before. How long had he been there? It didn't smell too bad, and there were no flies. Was he still alive when I entered his home? Had he been lying there—hoping that I was there to help him and save his life, only for me to instead rummage through his home as he lay there dying alone and in agony? Was the home his, or would the homeowner arrive to find a dead body in their house? I didn't see any framed photos during my search. That's not uncommon these days, though, with technology being what it is. If the man wasn't the homeowner, then who could he be? Did the homeowner kill him and go out to get the necessary supplies to hide or destroy a body? All the possible scenarios slam down, back to back to back, each only increasing the number of my questions rather than providing answers.

I want to know more. I need to know more. Has he been found yet? Who was he? What happened? Could I have helped?

There's a serial killer here in the South, one that no one has been able to identify. Many people believe he's still active, but no one is really sure. He is very concise and controlled, it seems, murdering individuals on an annual basis. He's struck all over this region: Mississippi, Alabama, Texas, and even here in Louisiana. Of course, they know when it's him because he has a calling card, or whatever they call it, the thing serial killers do to let you know they kill, well, serially.

The murderer doesn't leave anything physical on the body,

presumably so they can't trace it back to him, and as far as anyone knows, he doesn't take anything with him, which is a genius way to avoid being caught with incriminating evidence. No, instead he uses each victim's blood to draw a line across their forehead. If he does anything else, the media has never mentioned it.

I bet whoever created his notorious name thought they were pretty cute. Initially, different media news sites referred to him by a few names. The Artist, for the drawing of the line. The Expunger, because it was like he was crossing people off a list. The Firefighter, because he drew a red line. Ultimately, the media deemed him the Southern Slasher years ago. Somehow, it stuck, and that's what they call him. I wonder if he likes the name and thinks it fits, or if he would have preferred one of the other names.

I feel like I didn't see a line on the dead man's forehead. Of course, that doesn't mean no line was there. It's almost as if my mind cannot recall the details for fear of reliving the horrid ordeal. Technically, if the line wasn't there, that could mean I interrupted the killer before he was done.

I'm innately cautious, and I also overthink what I do a lot. So of course I'm doing it now. I've been so extremely cautious with choosing targets, and I hate that a hiccup this big has happened. I was cautious then, and I'm cautious even now. I don't want to search the internet in case someone has been watching me or the police ever trace any evidence back to me. I haven't done anything, but you've got to admit I look guilty as hell. I need to ensure that I don't do anything that could ever lead the police to question or suspect me.

One of my close friends works at the local police station, but it's not like she's a detective, so I'm not sure she'd even have access to any information for this case, and that's *if* they've found the body. I surely can't just text her out of the blue, asking oddly specific questions. But... I could text her a hello and reestablish an open line of communication in the hopes that our conversations will lead to something. I'm going to plant a seed. I grab my phone for the first time since I've gotten home, ignoring the few notifications I have and instead pulling up the text thread between Bianca and me.

As I do, I see the last time we texted was about a month ago. Yikes. I thought I considered her a good friend, but a surprising amount of time passed since we last spoke with one another. It's a good thing I'm reaching out. It almost makes sense for me to text her, since it's long overdue. I don't want to say, "Hey, missing you, just checking in," because we can't start a conversation like that. Not a proper one, anyway. So instead I text her, "Who was that guy you dated in high school again? The one with the mohawk? I think I saw him today!"

She doesn't have to know that I remember his name was Chris, and that I even recall we all referred to him as Chris the Crawfish Man. She has even less need to know I actually did see him recently, and that I didn't think to text her at the time. He stopped me at the grocery store, and we talked about what we'd been up to lately. I got the feeling he was flirting with me but was too shy to make the move. It was awkward once I realized, and I tried to dismiss him politely and go about my shopping. Really, I should have texted her when I saw him yet again across the street from the coffee shop, smoking a cigarette, but I ducked behind the counter before he could see me. Bianca and I could have talked about how weird it was to see him so frequently after not thinking about him for years. Now I'm having to use his appearances as an excuse to sneak back into her life.

I huff out a sigh and fall back onto my plush white sofa, attempting to ease some of the tension that is now ever-present in my body after today's events. Then another idea pops into my head. The news! I can easily turn on the local news or scroll on social media in the hopes of learning something about the man. The man whose body I found in a pool of blood earlier today. No wonder my body is as stiff as a board. I tense up every time I think about that man's corpse, and it's literally all I can think about.

How can I live like this? How do murderers live like this? It must stop, right? Reliving the day. The questions. The what-ifs? I don't know whether following the news will ease my conscience or exacerbate the dread, but it's about time I find out.

I turn on the TV and flip to the local news station, on which a pregnant broadcaster is commenting on the high temperatures. Nothing new there. That's Louisiana for you, always hot, and even more so in the summer months like we're in now. As I wait for the program to highlight any breaking news, or news in general, I open up my phone to see if anything has been shared or posted. Instead of searching directly for keywords like "murder," "killed," or "suspect," I just continue to pull my finger upward, hoping to stumble on a parish police alert or local news article. As I scroll, all I see are all the typical things you'd suspect, until I don't.

The Terrebonne Parish Sheriff's Office has a post, and I see the word "fatal," but soon after reading the caption, I realize it's just about a car accident.

Something like relief flashes throughout my body, but it doesn't last long as my thoughts begin to race again. Why are you relieved? You didn't kill him. Eventually they'll find him.

I'm not exactly sure why I feel so worried. I guess it's just because I've spent all this time trying to fly under the radar and not get caught, only to end up in even more trouble than I ever imagined. I really need to stop listening to true crime podcasts.

Just then, I see red flash across the TV screen out of the corner of my eye, and I direct my full attention to the screen as a news reporter appears there. I'm sure the color drains from my face, because she's standing in a familiar neighborhood, blue-and-red lights flashing and erasing shadows intermittently as they dance along the houses in the background. My mouth drops as the caption rolls by on the bottom of the screen.

Local Man Murdered.

Chapter 6

My obsession, as I imagine you could call it, started when I was dropping off a coffee delivery. The same car always passed mine, heading in the opposite direction every time. I got curious. I became speculative and began creating stories in my mind. Perhaps the driver's wife thought that he was at home, searching and applying for jobs online, but in reality, he waited for her to leave for work, giving her time to settle in and ensuring she wouldn't return home before he left to meet his mistress. The mistress was a woman he fell deeply in love with when they used to work together, which was coincidentally how he lost his job in the first place. Or maybe he was a stay-at-home dad with a standing playdate for his young son, who needed social interaction because he had behavioral issues and the pediatrician recommended it. Each Tuesday that I would pass the man on his way out, I'd imagine another storyline with him as the main character.

Then, Kristi gave me a whole Tuesday off for an annual check-up that I had scheduled, telling me that I had earned a day to myself. What I did with that day off was obvious. I went to watch the same man. I saw his home and, following him, finally beheld where he went every Tuesday. The excitement that flowed through my body was electric, and I shivered with delight as I pursued him. It didn't take long for me to discover that he was just going to the gym.

He pulled into the gym parking lot, and from my own parking spot, I watched him enter the glass-walled building, meet a muscular personal trainer, and shake his hand. I waited approximately two hours before my lanky subject exited the gym in a fresh pair of casual clothing, waving at the muscular man, who remained behind in the gym. Feeling like this outing was a bust, I continued to follow the slim man. All he did was drive to a local coffee shop. Instead of pulling into the drive-through, he stepped out of his car with a computer bag and walked inside. I waited in the parking lot again for another thirty minutes before I had to go to my appointment, which took a couple of hours. Out of curiosity, I passed by the coffee shop on my way home, and the lanky man's car was still there.

What started out as a thrilling adventure quickly turned into an uneventful outing. He wasn't doing anything exciting, and I had guessed nothing right! I had resolved that my imagination was far more elaborate than anything he actually did.

The following Tuesday came back around, and, like clock-work, I crossed that man's path as he left for his gym session with his personal trainer. My subject was none the wiser that the woman driving the vehicle in the opposing lane had followed him a week ago. From tracking him last week, I now knew something new about him—where his house was. I drove past it slowly, observing that the house had no car in the driveway or one of those doorbell cameras, and then an idea sparked. An idea that would change the way in which I was nosy.

I hadn't gotten the level of satisfaction that I was hoping to receive in my sporadic adventures, so I decided to take this one up a notch. I knew that he wouldn't be home, so I would see if I could find anything better by digging through his house.

I had waited another week, and then, instead of taking my lunch, I decided to break into the lanky man's house. Breaking in sounds serious, but it was what I had to do. I don't know him; I had no reason to be in his home, and I literally had to pick the lock on his door, a useful skill I had learned from my friend Bianca during her rebellious teenage years.

I intended to give myself just an hour. Upon entering the house and after stepping over the threshold, my life flashed before me as something raced across the room. Regret washed over me instantly. This idea was reckless, and I would be in so much trouble. I then saw the fast-moving blob again, directed my attention toward it, and discovered that it was a cat. That was when I began to formulate my no-pets rule, especially for dogs.

I spent my entire lunch hour rummaging through his office and bedroom to learn that the lanky man was named Dean and that he did indeed have some secrets to hide after all. My initial house hunt uncovered some unique finds—creepy porcelain dolls adorning shelves in a spare bedroom, what appeared to be a hex bag under the master bedroom's mattress, and an assortment of men and women's shoes varying from adult size seven to adult size eleven, all for the right foot. Those discoveries evoked more questions in me, obviously. The findings were what I needed to satiate my thirst for discovery and curiosity. On Dean's dresser, I also found a keychain that read, "I like big trucks and big butts," which I considered taking home to my boyfriend at the time. I decided not to so I could avoid questions about where I'd obtained it. Right then, I created another one of my rules: Don't take anything.

In that moment, I also realized that just because I shouldn't take anything didn't prevent me from still having a little more fun. So on my way out the door, I took the keychain from the bedroom and placed it near the couch in the living room.

* * *

Should I call in sick to work? One of the many thoughts I struggle with. Do I text Kristi so she knows to expect my absence, adjust the schedule, and call in reinforcements? If I do, I'll likely just wake up in a panic to see the sunlight streaming past the curtains and into my room and then find myself unable to go back to sleep after a fitful night of unrest. I may as well go on as normal with my life. I can't alert anybody to a change in my personality or schedule, since people may begin to ask questions, connect the dots, and make accusations.

I won't skip work just to lie in bed, staring at the white rectangles that line my ceiling, sinking deeper into my thoughts. I'll shake off this feeling and put on a brave face. Try to go back to normal.

I create a mantra then. *You did nothing wrong.*

In the eyes of the law, sure, I was breaking and entering, but I didn't hurt that man. He's not dead because of me. So I can't let his death bog me down and impact my life any longer.

Therefore, I repeat my mantra that night as I go about ignoring the news and preparing for bed. I eat a small frozen meal so that I don't have to bother with dishes, and I shower and try to start getting ready for bed as if nothing is awry.

I know it will be difficult to fall asleep with the way my mind has been racing, so I decide to read a book, hoping that it'll distract me and prepare me for what I'm sure will be a restless night.

Before I can even open my book, my phone chimes from the bedside table where it's charging. I grab the device to see that Bianca has replied to my message.

BeeOnka: *OMG! No, stop! Wow, I'm speechless. We should catch up soon! It's been too long.*

Typically, when I get a text like this, I wonder if the person saying it is being serious or if they're just being nice and don't mean it. Regardless of whether the invitation is authentic or not, I send her my reply.

Zoey: *Yes, let's put it on the calendar now. Are you free Thursday?*

BeeOnka: *Yes! Loony Bin for 7?*

I send her a thumbs-up before settling back into bed for a night that may very well be sleepless.

Chapter 7

My next victim, as I like to refer to the houses I choose, isn't the best option for what I have in store. Only because of a small dent in my carefully curated process.

There's no denying that I've put a lot of time into observing it, and I can't let all the effort go to waste. I could call it off, but then I'd have to scout another house, and that could take weeks. I'm eager to fulfill my treacherous desires. I can't call this action reckless, because I have done a lot of research on the chosen home. I've done this before, so I have a carefully conceived plan. The only problem is a minor discrepancy in the home's schedule that took place a couple of weeks ago, which worries me and makes me think it could lead to something that could interfere.

This house, a small brick home in the middle of a rather long street, has been my intended victim for weeks now. Initially, what I do is begin to pass by and watch a home that I consider to be ideal. Now I may observe more than one house at this stage of scouting, if I spot additional contenders.

I then escalate things, and I start to blend in as a member of the community in the evenings, "exercising" by walking or jogging down the street or even just driving by with the magnets from work still displayed on my car. As the process goes on, I tend to weed out candidates until I can narrow them down to the perfect target.

After a week of monitoring in this manner, I start parking on the street and watching the chosen home. To avoid drawing suspicion, I never do this on the same day or time. Finally, for the last three weeks of my mission, I park on the street on the same weekday and at the same time I plan to enter the home. I do this to ensure the homeowner keeps a consistent schedule, as well as for neighbors and community members.

Ideally, there is very little foot traffic or car travel, thus diminishing my chances of being seen and recognized on the day I intend to commit my crime. My objective during these scouting missions is always the same: ensuring the house is unoccupied within the time frame I plan to trespass.

My next target was chosen in just the same way I chose them in the past. The only issue with this house is that at one point in my scouting, someone interrupted the consistent schedule. That's why I'm so cautious. If this were to happen during my invasion, well, I could be caught.

I didn't like that development, and I'd called off a target before when it happened. I just hate that it happened so late in the process for this one. So instead of aborting and scrapping the whole plan, I decided to proceed and add an extra week of monitoring.

The interruption in an otherwise consistent schedule was the appearance of a landscaper. Every day during the week, the house sat lonely and isolated, beckoning me. The home was not equipped with a garage, so the owner's presence would be easily determined by the absence or presence of a car in the driveway.

I liked that the house wasn't near a stop sign, so that no one would have a reason to stop unless they lived in a nearby home. Through investigation, I determined that the mail carrier in this neighborhood passed late in the afternoon. Also, many older people appeared to live here in Sugar Garden, too, so there weren't many joggers or dog walkers.

Neither the owner nor their neighbor had a freshly manicured lawn, but theirs weren't alarmingly overgrown, indicating no hired help. So I was confused when a lawn care truck and trailer arrived on what was to be my last week of stalking.

I watched them from my parked car. The burly man who emerged from the truck did not unload it and begin cutting the grass. No, instead I watched him as he placed a note on the door of my target's house and walked slowly back to the vehicle. Rather than getting back in, the tall man turned around, walked next door to the neighbor's house, and left what appeared to be another note on its door as well.

I waited for the guy to leave and allowed a gracious amount of time before I walked up to each door to investigate further. I had already determined that none of the houses in this area had a doorbell camera. I could only assume that the occupants felt safe and secure nestled in the middle of the subdivision. Or that some of them were too old to understand how those popular digital doorbell cameras worked.

Obviously, that little hiccup put a dent in my plan. I couldn't have that guy show up again and spoil my fun, so I had to decide how I would proceed. Seeing what was written on those notes would be helpful, but was it worth the risk inherent in approaching the homes?

I determined that to truly decide whether it was safer to call it off or to proceed, I'd have to know what those notes said. I decided to walk to the neighbor's house first. I waited in my car for a moment, wanting to make sure that not too many cars were passing through. None of the neighbors nearby appeared to be outside either. I had to fight the urge to speed to each door. I would get back to my car quicker, but it would ring alarm bells if anyone were to see me. Casual and cool was the way to go. I had to look like I belonged there and walk around with confidence.

I eased myself out of the car and looked both ways before I crossed the street. I did it for safety—safety in passing the road and to ensure I wasn't being watched. I walked leisurely up the neighbor's narrow sidewalk and straight to their disheveled blue door, the paint peeling in spots. I pretended to knock as I skimmed the note.

The name Ledet's Landscaping appeared in bold letters, accompanied by a phone number. Below, someone had scribbled by hand, "Just passing by. Give me a call if you'd be interested."

I then acted as if no one had answered the door and pretended to be disappointed before returning to my car. Had to put on a show just on the off chance that someone was watching me. Right as I reached the street, I turned around and looked at my target's house. I wanted it to appear as if my going there was a last-ditch effort to get ahold of their neighbor. Again, I strolled casually up to my target's solid red door, not nearly as unkempt as the one I just left. I lifted my balled fist to feign a knock and read the note. It was the same business card but with a different message written below:

"You still owe me the balance from last summer."

I let out a sigh of relief, and just for looks, I walked straight toward the neighbor on the other side of the house with a clean white door. Once again, I pretended to knock before returning quickly to my car.

I could deal with this. It wasn't bad enough to concern me. Based on the overall condition of the yard and house that belonged to the neighbor who received the note, I doubted they'd be interested in hiring for lawn maintenance. As for my target, if the guy was just looking to collect a debt from last summer, I doubted he'd come around again and interrupt me.

Just in case, I decided to add another week but otherwise proceed as usual.

The last week of monitoring was the previous week, although it was supposed to be invasion time. Now, this week, I get to proceed with my favorite part now that I've determined that the lawn care thing was a freak accident and unlikely to happen again.

Chapter 8

The next day, I go through the morning, performing my job on autopilot, putting in extra work to speak to others so my melancholy mood isn't too obvious. I make all my deliveries, stopping here and there to scroll social media for news updates, only to find none. They haven't even released the dead man's name, which I assume is because the investigation is ongoing. During my shift, I get verification of the matter when I drive by his house and witness police cars and barrier tape around it. I try not to make my presence too apparent as I pass, averting my eyes more than analyzing the scene. They say the killer returns to the scene of the crime, so I don't want anyone to see me and think that that's the case.

Nope, not me. I'm only here to deliver some delicious iced coffee. Orders that were placed even before this happened. Well, if anyone stops me and asks, that's what I'll say.

Of course, after seeing the active investigation on full display, my imagination takes flight, creating imaginary suspects based on what little information I have. Well, I have more information than the public does, since I was there and saw the body.

I have a feeling the news will start speculating that the Southern Slasher orchestrated this murder. According to a murder mystery podcast I listened to recently, he's about due to commit his next crime. But I have the inside scoop. I saw more than what the media saw.

The whole thing is a blur to me now that I've had time to sit with it—finding the body. I think my mind is trying to forget about it, push it into a mental closet so I can't remember the discovery. Even so, I feel like I didn't see a line on the man's forehead. Of course, it doesn't mean that the line wasn't there. Technically, if the line wasn't there, that could mean I interrupted the killer before he was finished.

In that case... the killer could have seen me. They might begin to stalk me like I stalk homes, and they may even put me on the list of potential victims. No one knows how or why he chooses his victims, so it's not outside the realm of possibility.

I know I can't be the first person to think this, so it's only a matter of time before the theory starts circulating. Who really knows how the guy died? Maybe he fell and busted his head on the corner of the counter. I've heard of things like that happening... police looking into a suspicious death in which the body was found in a bloodbath, only to discover it was a freak accident once the investigation is completed.

Regardless, I know people will be talking. I live in a small town where things like murder and serial killers just don't happen.

I'm looking forward to seeing Bianca tomorrow. She's just a desk sergeant at the police station, but I hope I can easily get her to spill some details on the case, if she has any. It's totally normal and reasonable to inquire. Around here, I'm sure I won't be the only one asking questions. People tend to talk in our small community, spreading truth and rumors alike.

If all goes well, the department will have time to collect as much data as possible by the time Bianca and I meet up. I want the victim's name, the suspects, the motive, the cause of death—everything. I won't be too obvious about my desires, though, and I'll have to take what I can get without arousing suspicion, assuming she knows anything. I've never worked in a police department, but I've watched some TV shows. I don't think it's too far-fetched to assume she may know something about the case, especially considering how the gossip is around here and across southern Louisiana.

As the day goes on, my guilt begins to lessen. I'm not completely unburdened by any means, but that guilt feels lighter and lighter. I was just in the wrong place at the wrong time. Who knows if the alleviation is my brain's way of trying to protect me, if I'm doing a good job convincing myself, or if I actually feel better about the whole thing now that some time has passed? Sure, I break into people's homes. I may need to re-evaluate that aspect of my life, or at least take a break from trespassing. I'm sure I can fulfill my unusual thirst for drama in some other way, but for now, I've seen a dead body, and that's enough drama to last a lifetime.

Chapter 9

When I pull up to the Loony Bin, the parking lot is nearly empty. With such a crass name, it's a miracle the place is still open. I'm not sure why it's named that, but the locals come here regardless. Maybe just so they can say, quirkily, "I'm headed to the Loony Bin," when, in reality, they're just going out for drinks. This little pub, nestled in downtown Houma, truly caters to our more eccentric locals, who have special interests like video games and anime TV shows.

I've always liked this small establishment, and I'm not ashamed to admit that I'm different. I've never been the popular girl on the dance team, the pothead who gets stoned, or even the nerdy girl. Since my young adult years, I've been comfortable and unjudged, which has allowed me to continue being myself, since I'm just uniquely me. I was never teased, nor did I ever experience a rough patch in adolescence, unlike Bianca. She was rebellious when we were younger and even had a brief stint in juvenile detention for some typical reckless teenage behavior. I actually met my ex through her following her release from juvie. He was one of the new edgy friends she'd made during her short time there.

My high school friends and I found ourselves here after we became old enough to drink around eight years ago. While most of the college kids would go to the bars and clubs, we would come here to sit and make memories.

I imagine that's why Bianca's chosen to meet here. I bet when she got the text from me that this was the first place that popped into her mind. It's still kind of early, but it's also Thursday, so I'm sure as the night goes on, the Loony Bin will get busier and busier. I grab my purse as I step out of the car and walk toward the glass double doors, my jeans scraping the ground as I go. It's too hot to wear jeans outside, but since we'll be spending most of the time inside the building, I figure I'll be okay. The sky is in the middle of its transition from sunny day to dark night, so on the horizon, I see the dim curtain falling upon neon pink-and-orange clouds. Off in the distance, I smell a hint of smoked meat.

When I open the door, the bell chimes, notifying the bar's few occupants of my arrival. As I walk in, a head looks up from a booth on the right, and Bianca's smiling eyes greet me as she exits the booth. I rush to her, and we embrace. I needed this hug. A hug from an old and true friend who knows that I'm a good person. A friend who has always loved me and will continue to love me no matter how much time passes between each reunion.

Once we separate, I hold her forearms and study her. She still looks just as she did when we were kids, with her chubby cheeks, straight blond hair, and chestnut-colored eyes that rest gently above her freckled nose. I give her a smile as I let her go and shimmy into the booth seat, and she does the same across from me.

"I ordered you a surprise drink," she says with a tilt of her head.

My smile widens as she proves how well she knows my love

for surprises.

"You. Know. Me." I say, emphasizing each word. She bursts into laughter, and I join her, not having to fake the joy that I feel at this moment.

"I'll never forget that," she tells me as she slaps her hand on the table lightly.

It's one of our many inside jokes. This one comes from an encounter I had with a customer when Bianca and I worked at a restaurant together in high school. A customer had accused me of rudeness, and I became so defensive that I barked, "I wouldn't do that. *You know me!*" to everyone in the kitchen after the incident occurred. At the time, I felt frustrated. Now, though, we laugh about it at every opportunity. That I was defending my kindness with aggression was kind of hilarious.

"You and me both," I tell her.

I could use this opportunity to transition into talking about our respective jobs, but I don't want to seem too eager, so I don't. I'll let her lead the conversation, since I'm sure the topic will come up eventually. It'll be even less suspect if she talks about work first without my having to mention it.

"It was a great idea to come here! So many memories of this place," I say as I glance around at the walls, which are adorned with local band posters and eccentric illustrations of an assortment of popular video games.

"Right!? I mean, like, when's the last time we came here? We were overdue for this."

"Very true. Crazy to think how, at that age, we were wondering about what we'd be doing now."

"I never would have thought I'd work at the police station, that's for sure."

Yes, she said it first. That's my in.

"At least you're not, like, a cop or a detective," I say. "While that may be an interesting job, I can see it being a difficult and time-consuming one."

"Yep. I feel like I get the best of both worlds, in a sense. I hear about the calls and the cases, but I get to work a nine-to-five with no obligation to work myself to death, ya know?"

I nod.

"For instance, this new case... I know your nosy self knows the one I'm talking about," she says as she raises her eyebrows at me. "Well, this case will be taking up *all* their time. It doesn't happen often, something like that, but when it does, they put in as much time as they can to get the victim justice."

I have no idea what to do here. Feign ignorance and pretend I am clueless about what she means? I feel like doing that would be more obvious than telling her directly that I am aware of what she is describing.

"Oh yeah, I saw that," I decide to say, since it feels like the safest option for proceeding with the conversation. Before she can move on to another topic, I say, "Stuff like that never happens around here. You probably don't know all that much about the nitty-gritty, though, right?"

Perhaps if I attack her ego passively-aggressively, she'll get defensive and tell me everything she knows to prove me wrong.

"Girl, you'd be surprised what a little ol' desk sergeant hears about around here. I can practically see the evidence board from my desk."

"No way! Like what?" I ask, averting my eyes, trying not to appear too eager.

"Well," she says, pausing to look around before turning back to face me, "that guy was definitely murdered. The crime scene photos are atrocious. They've mentioned the Southern Slasher, but if it was him, he forgot to leave his signature. They're canvasing the area now and looking for possible suspects, but they don't have anyone yet. I don't know what's worse, the serial killer or a random act of violence from someone in town," she says, shaking her head in disapproval.

"Wow, and you know all that just from being in the same building. Look at you! You could almost join the team as a detective," I say in an attempt to flatter her.

I watch as sweat glistens on her forehead, and I realize suddenly that she may regret leaking this information to me.

"I really shouldn't be talking about it, but you and I have been friends for years, and I can trust you not to tell anyone, right?" she asks me with a pleading look in her eyes.

"Of course! I won't tell a soul! I know how people get around here when they hear stuff like this. I don't want to stoke the fire."

I appreciate what she's told me so far, and I'm lucky I've gotten as much information from her as I have. I don't expect her to tell me anything else. Not now, anyway.

She needs to know that she can trust me with more information as it comes to light. She doesn't have to worry about discussing those crime scene photos, though. I was there right before they were even taken.

Chapter 10

One would think that after talking to Bianca, my nerves would have settled, but instead, the conversation has brought the fear back into me. I just can't get over this whole thing. I'm not sure how I can live like this, with this pressure weighing down on me all the time.

I can't stop thinking about how I wasn't supposed to be there. I have no idea what truly happened. Did I do the right thing? Could I have done more to save him? Was I almost the next victim? May I still end up on some sicko's hit list? The heaviness of all the possible consequences that stem from one decision of mine is almost insurmountable.

I invited Bianca over today so that I could see her again. I usually look forward to lounging around on the weekends, maybe even doing some detailed cleaning around the house, but not this weekend. I couldn't bear being alone with my thoughts any longer. I also invited a couple of other friends of ours from high school, Sierra and Kaci. I was hoping that hosting a few of them would keep my mind off things and that they'd leave a mess so I could busy myself with cleaning.

Also, in doing things this way, Bianca won't think I'm fishing for information either. She'll think that it's what everyone else thinks it is—a girls' night.

In reality, it's just me trying to kill two birds with one stone. The old, unbothered me would have put together a personalized charcuterie board full of my friends' favorite snacks, or suggested that we do one of those cute parties in which we all bring a movie-inspired cocktail. Not tonight. I don't have it in me, and I hope that they don't notice. To try to mask my inability to host a fun get-together, I stopped at the local grocery store and grabbed a large adult snack pack (sandwich-meat slices, squares of cheese, and crackers). As I arrange all the food on one of my smaller wooden boards, I hear a knock at the door. I leave everything as it is and rush toward my front door.

I open it to find Bianca's smiling face.

"I couldn't get here fast enough! I brought some white wine for us. I figured that we could try to pretend to be classy tonight," she says as she saunters past me and places the wine on the island in the kitchen.

She's dressed casually tonight, as am I, in a pair of athleisure pants and a T-shirt. She kicks off her tennis shoes and pours us each a glass of wine, the sweet smell unleashed simultaneously with the sound of the popped cork. Another knock at the door sounds just as she pushes my glass across the island and toward me.

"Better pour two more," I tell her as I walk toward the door.

Before I can even reach it, the door flies open, and Sierra squeals with delight, running at me at full force. She envelops me in a hug, and I savor the deep pressure it provides.

"Okay," she says as she pulls away from me, still holding onto my shoulders while looking me directly in the eye. "It's about time we do something like this! I go and have a kid and you guys just think we can't have fun anymore?"

"Umm, excuse you," Kaci says as she walks through and then closes the door, "but I had a kid first and they still hung out with me. It must just be you."

Kaci nudges Sierra's shoulder with her elbow to indicate she's not serious before pulling me into a hug. I suddenly hear footsteps running toward me from the kitchen and quickly feel Bianca's arms wrap around me from behind.

"Group hug without me?" Sierra screams before trying to wrap her long, thin arms around the three of us.

I want to cry at my friends' show of affection. I want to break down right here and weep endlessly, but I can't. Instead, I try to join in on their giggles, welcoming the hug and instead focusing on the happiness that my companions bring to my life.

You'd think we never see one another, and I guess, in a way, that's kind of true. We've been friends since high school, and I know how lucky we are to have made it out of there without losing that level of intimacy to time. We all have jobs, and some of us have kids. Boyfriends get in the way too. Well, for me they do.

For some reason, when I have a boyfriend, even at twenty-nine years old, I get all obsessed and attached. That might even be why I can't keep one around long enough to marry me. I know it's bad, and I truly can't help it. As soon as I have a boyfriend, all I want to do is hang out with him, and I manage to pull myself away for work, but that's it.

My friends know how I am, so I'm glad they haven't kicked me to the curb. They just wait for me to have time for them again. Which usually happens once my flavor of the month gets sick of me and dumps me.

With all that life has to give, my friends and I don't hang out much. Truly, you could cast blame on any one of us. It's crazy that we all live in the same town and can't make the time to get together.

Regardless, we're here now, and even though I say "we need to do this more often" every time, it's true.

I grab my glass and a clean one for Sierra as Bianca follows me to grab both hers and one for Kaci. We all go and sit around the coffee table in my living room, but just as I put my glass down and prepare to sit, I remember to run to the kitchen and scoop up the snack-laden board.

"Nothing much today. Just a little something," I say as I place it down on the table.

"Aw, that'll work!" Sierra says with a laugh. That's Sierra. She is always unapologetically her loud and bubbly self.

As she sits next to Kaci, it's easy to see why they often get mistaken for sisters. Coincidentally, they have the same dark brown hair; Sierra's is straight and thin, while Kaci's is wavy and thick. The similarity isn't only in their hair. They have the same fair skin and dark eyes, although Sierra is taller and thinner than Kaci.

Their personalities, though—well, those are exact opposites. Kaci is somber and brooding, while Sierra is jovial and sprightly. Meanwhile, Bianca and I have very similar personalities. We all match up well together, the four of us. How many people can say they have a close group of four friends? Well, we could be closer. We need to be from here on out.

At first, we become engrossed in learning about what everyone's been doing recently. I can blend into the background easily, since I don't have a child or boyfriend to share anecdotes about. So I just listen happily to Sierra and Kaci talk about their kids and Bianca discuss her fiancé and dog. They poke fun at me, too, laughing over who was more obsessed with the other—me or my ex, Lucas.

They're familiar with him, especially since I only met him because of Bianca. We were so good together, until we weren't, although our breakup wasn't due to anything either of us had done wrong.

I nod, laughing along as we talk. Even if I don't learn anything from Bianca tonight, this small get-together is exactly what I've needed. I think I can live with this guilt if I can get monthly interactions with my three best friends. Yes, I'm calling them my best friends, because this is going to keep happening no matter what else comes our way. I have no excuse for having been such a distant friend to them, and they deserve better from me. I can be more present. I want their kids to refer to me as Taunte Zoey, rather than just "Mom's friend."

"Yikes, do you think we'll have to be extra-careful when we leave tonight?" Kaci asks us, pulling me from my thoughts.

"Right? There could be a serial killer on the loose. I know that he has a routine he usually follows, but I also have seen my fair share of crime documentaries, and those crazies don't always stick to it. They can escalate!" Sierra says as she brushes crumbs off her T-shirt.

"You're right. I don't want to think about it like that, but you have to with it happening so close to home," I say with a grimace.

"I'm not supposed to say anything," Bianca says softly, possibly hoping we wouldn't hear her comment and continue without her input. But it has the opposite effect. We all turn toward her and wait quietly for her to elaborate.

She tilts her head down and looks at us from beneath hooded eyes.

"It might not be a serial killer after all. They have a suspect."

My eyes widen in shock. Is it me? It can't be me. She wouldn't be here, right? She wouldn't have said that if that were the case. God, I hope it's someone else. I hope they find the actual killer and don't set their sights on me, an innocent bystander.

"Spit it out. Please don't tell us it's someone we know?" Sierra says, no longer tolerating the long silence that has followed Bianca's statement.

"I don't think y'all do. I don't want to say his name. I'm too paranoid. They haven't even found him yet. It's all very new. I'd hate to tell you guys and then rumors spread and his reputation gets tarnished for nothing," she says hurriedly, hardly taking a breath in between sentences.

Relief floods through me. I'm not the suspect. She said "him," and I don't think she'd lie to me. Rather than showing the relief that I feel, I contribute to the mania.

"They can't find him?" I say with alarm in my voice.

"Y'all, I'm serious," Bianca responds. "Can we not talk about it anymore? I shouldn't have said anything. They have a suspect. We don't know him. Well, I'm pretty sure we don't. They haven't been able to locate him for questioning yet. Please. Let's leave it at that."

"So what you're saying is that we don't have to be afraid of a serial killer, just a random killer who is evading capture? Wow! That makes me feel better," Kaci says, rolling her eyes and dropping her shoulders.

"Ugh. Y'all just go straight home after this! Don't talk to strangers. It was probably some kind of domestic dispute gone wrong. It's still early stages, so nothing is concrete," Bianca says, trying to reassure us.

"I get it, Bianca," I say. "It's like, if you tell us he left a note in the guy's mouth, and we go spreading that to the public... the police will know there's a leak, which might delay finding the real murderer. You can't give us information and jeopardize things. Gossiping with us isn't worth losing your job over." I place my hand on her arm in an attempt to calm her. I want her to understand she can trust me.

She sighs with relief.

"Yes. You guys know I'd tell you if I were concerned for your safety, but I really think it was a fluke and y'all will be okay. Trust me. I promise to discuss this with you after everything is over. I know I'm just a glorified receptionist, but I love my job, and I can't risk losing it," she says.

I raise my hands in the air in a gesture of surrender.

"Deal. Right, guys? We'll lay off," I say, looking at the others, hoping to see them nod.

Unanimously, they reply with a reluctant mumble of "okay."

"Anybody know any good over-the-counter hemorrhoid creams?" Sierra asks with a laugh, apparently trying to change the subject.

Although we never ran out of things to talk about, the evening eventually wound down, and it was finally time for my friends to go.

"As I don't have to rush home to snuggle sweet babies,"

Bianca says as she looks toward Kaci and Sierra, "I'll hang behind a second and help tidy up."

"Thanks, B!" Sierra mumbles into her ear as she hugs her goodbye, while Kaci embraces me.

Sierra pulls back from Bianca and grabs hold of me as Kaci takes the spot in Bianca's arms.

"This was so fun! See you soon, Zoey. Thanks for the invite!" Sierra says.

"What she said," Kaci says as she and Sierra walk out my front door.

"Y'all be safe!" I yell while they venture out into the humid night. The hot air rushes in from outside and quickly reaches my cheek.

"Thanks so much for staying to help clean," I say to Bianca as I close the door and join her in the kitchen.

"Of course! It's the least I could do. Thanks for having us over," she says as she opens the dishwasher to put away our dirty glasses. Meanwhile, I scrape what little food is left on the board into the trash can.

Just then, I notice the clock on the kitchen wall is upside down. Confusion rushes through me.

"B, did you guys do that to mess with me?" I ask, pointing at the clock.

"No! I noticed it was like that when I walked in earlier. I forgot to ask you about it."

A chill zooms through my entire body as I stand still, staring at the clock.

"Thanks for being so understanding earlier," she says without looking me in the eye, pulling me out of my trance.

"I absolutely get it."

"You know how people like to talk around here, and as much

as I trust y'all, I just don't want to risk anything being made too public."

I smile to ease her worry.

"Can't deny that I'm nosy, though. *You know me.*"

She laughs with me and pulls me in for a hug.

"It's just some lawn care guy. Who knows what will come of all this? What if he didn't even do it? They haven't questioned him yet. But I'd feel so bad if it got out and he lost all of his business only to find out he did nothing wrong."

I stare at her with wide eyes but not for the reason she thinks.

"Oops. Pretend I didn't say that?" she asks me, lifting an eyebrow in question.

I have to relax my face consciously and force a smile.

"Say what?" I ask with a wink. "Seriously, it's no big deal. You don't even have to tell me his company name or whatever. We can leave him in anonymity," I tell her as I usher her out the front door.

I don't need to ask, though, since I am certain of whom she is speaking. After all, I saw him at the victim's house before his murder.

Chapter 12

I didn't mean to kill him. As I dream, I see the whole thing happen in bursts. I didn't go there with the intent of hurting him. Deep down and even superficially, that's not the kind of person I am. I'm sure all people think they're good, or at least most of them do. No—I haven't done anything exceptional for anybody in my life at any point in time, but that doesn't make me a horrible person. Again, I don't ever choose to do something that I know will hurt someone. Sometimes I'm not at my best. Sometimes, I don't even feel like myself. In those moments, it isn't me doing anything bad. More like a part of me that I can't control.

There is no arguing the point, no matter how much I may try to defend my character to myself. Killing him makes me a horrible person. I am now and will always be a terrible person, regardless of how I choose to act in the light of day, in which no one knows what I've done. No one sees the scars left on my soul. The burden is now only mine to bear.

Is it not enough that I think about it all day? Now I must be plagued in my sleep as well? My dreams are haunting, character-ized by bursts of tumultuous memories, billowing clouds of black smoke, and chilling sounds: a thud, the rattling of a cage, the beat of my racing heart.

The vivid dream is almost always the same, and I often awake in a sheen of sweat—stuck to my sheets. When I manage to fall back asleep, it only ever continues. Never disappears. It's driving me insane, I fear.

He didn't like that I went to his house. He was upset. He yelled at me. Demanded to know why I was there. I didn't have an answer.

His reaction stunned me; I froze. I didn't know what to do. What to say.

Black. Dark and impenetrable. A wall of fog, possibly my mind's attempt to hide the traumatic memory?

It doesn't last long. Images break through. The smoke dissipates. An image emerges, the fog clearing to allow me to watch my sins play out in a macabre performance. He's closer now. His face is inches from mine. I feel his spit hitting my face as he yells at me. I'm scared.

Black. Nothingness stretching on and on and on....

He's on the floor, blood seeping from his head wound. Spreading slowly across the white tiles.

The scene vanishes quickly behind a curtain of inky blackness. Quiet. Every dream feels like this. Every night is the same. Every day I'm awake but living a nightmare.

I reside here now in darkness. Every day is gloomy. My soul is now tormented by what I've done. I can almost forget what happened in the gloom. In the absence of all light.

Chapter 13

After Bianca left, I sat in my living room, staring at the clock on the wall, my mouth so dry I could taste it. I was left racking my brain for reasons why the clock was left that way. How long had it been like that? I sat for a while, wondering when was the last time I had used it to tell the hour.

Really, it's more for decoration. When I want to know the time, I typically glance at my smartwatch, or just open my phone.

I went to bed without any answers and woke up with more questions. Was anything else in my home out of place? Did I move the clock and forget? Did Bianca lie about changing its position?

And the scariest thought of all...

Is someone doing to me what I do to them after invading their home?

I woke up in a panic. Now I've been staring into space ever since. If someone was here and left behind a camera to spy on me, they'd surely think I'd gone mad.

Yikes. Can they see me? My messy hair while I lounge in my oversized T-shirt and boxers, appearing like a zombie? What else have they seen?

No, no, no.

There must be a rational explanation. There has to be. My sanity can't take much more of this onslaught of negative thoughts.

Think positive. I'll use my last day off to clean the house, and as I do, I'll look for hidden cameras. There. If they're watching me—if there is a *they*—they'll see me cleaning. If I identify a camera, I'll ignore it and formulate a plan from there. In the best-case scenario, I'm just paranoid.

After all, I enter people's houses and violate their privacy, but I'd never watch them in their homes. I have morals. That's painfully obvious the more I ruminate on the events of the past week. If I didn't have morals, then I wouldn't feel so dang bad for doing nothing wrong.

I go about cleaning the house, stopping briefly only to brush my teeth and freshen up my mouth with minty toothpaste. I play some music, more to fill the silence than to enjoy the sound. As I go about dusting and sweeping, I'm hyperaware of every item in my house. I search secretly for cameras or microphones, pretending to hum along to the music, ensuring my gaze doesn't linger too long on any one area. The task is tedious, but having two things to do at once is a reprieve from the constant morose thoughts.

Quickly and happily, I lose myself in the chore, racing about my house from end to end. The overpowering scent of cleaning products follows me throughout the house. When I'm finally finished, I haven't located a single camera or microphone.

I'm relieved, and I'm also ashamed that I was so paranoid. I found no other objects moved in the house, and I still have no explanation for the shifting of the clock's placement, but I am choosing this moment to determine that *it's nothing.*

I've been so out of my head lately, I wouldn't put it past me to be the culprit. For all I know, I get distracted and lost in thought so often that I'll find something else misplaced or rearranged tomorrow. I've never done that before, but there's a first time for everything.

After all, it's something I do to my victims. It's not an unusual thing for me to do to others, and so maybe I've begun subconsciously to do it to myself. I feel like that could be a completely plausible explanation for what happened with the clock. Almost like a habit.

One could theorize that it's my psyche trying to regulate itself, or some psychiatric mumbo jumbo. I don't know for sure; that was obviously never my department.

I sweep the final pile of dust from the floor into the dustpan, which I then empty into the nearly full trash can. This will be my last chore. Then I can try to find normalcy in scrolling through social media whilst I rot away on the couch.

As I walk outside, the searing Louisiana heat quickly begins to bake my skin. I rush to the bin and throw away the trash, my fuzzy slippers grating across the pavement as I go. Returning to the door, I notice a note on the frame that I must have missed when I walked out.

The speed with which I've been moving comes to a dead halt as I flash back to the day that the landscaper left those notes on the doors.

Has he found me? Goose bumps spread across my skin despite the sun's rays beating down on me.

I stand there, gawking at the note. I look around then, turning my whole body and slowly taking in my surroundings. No one appears to be watching me; in fact, the street is eerily silent.

Quinn's house on the right is quiet, as is the house on my left. That neighbor was released from jail recently, but he hadn't been imprisoned for anything too sinister. He was caught possessing drugs, which didn't strike me as unusual, since Eric had always been a little strange.

I walk toward the door, grab the note, and scurry inside. I lean my back against the door as I close it and pull the note up to eye level to read what it says.

I'm watching you.

That's it. Nothing else. It's not a business card like the others, but that doesn't mean it's not from the same guy. Doesn't mean it is either.

Jesus. Why me? Why, of all people, is this happening to me!?

Then another chilling thought hits me. What if he tells the police that I killed that man? Or worse—what if he kills me next?

I look at the clock, now hanging right side up, and back down at the note. It can't be a coincidence, can it?

I'm going to go crazy from all these tormenting thoughts. I'll be paranoid for the rest of my life, that's for sure.

I drop to the floor then, my pink slippers falling off as I slide down the door. I throw my head back in anguish, knocking it on the door as I do, before my tears begin to fall uncontrollably. This is miserable. Maybe it would be better if he killed me—that way I wouldn't have to go on living like this.

Chapter 14

As I deliver my orders the next day, my thoughts continue to suffocate me. The intoxicating aroma and intense flavors of my morning coffee do nothing to dispel the stress. It's my new normal.

Surely, I must go to the police to seek protection from the killer. But if I do, I run the risk of making myself a suspect. I'd basically be serving myself up on a silver platter.

It's like that story that went viral about the man who was convicted of a crime simply because he was the only suspect. He was eventually cleared with the discovery of new DNA evidence, but by the time it came to light, it was far too late. He had spent years in jail, and his reputation was tarnished beyond repair. Years of his life, gone. Years he would never get back.

Hypothetically, I could go to the police station to tell the cops I'm worried about my safety. Of course, they're going to ask questions, and I'll have to tell them why I feel threatened. They won't just take my word for it and send a patrol car to watch out for me for the foreseeable future. It doesn't work like that. I'd have to tell them about the note, the clock on the wall, and the fact that I was in the house with a dead body and didn't call to report it.

Sure, I saw the lawn care guy there, and I could accuse him of killing the guy and threatening me. Best-case scenario, they're like, "Yeah, you're right—he's guilty," but then I still have to suffer the repercussions of my actions. I'm sure the statute of limitations hasn't passed on my home invasion. So then I go to jail, pay a fine, or have something nefarious put on my record. Talking to the police wouldn't even solve the problem; it would just make more problems.

I want to go to the police to feel safe and forget about all of this, but going to the police would not do that for me. Really, my choice is made for me. I just have to wait this whole thing out. As soon as they find the killer and convict them of the murder, I can be at peace, knowing that the homeowner was already dead when I got there; there was nothing I could have done to save him, and I was not the one who killed him.

Truly, I need to be more worried about the clock in my house having moved. That threat is more concrete than the hypothetical scenarios that always infiltrate my rational thoughts. There is likely someone watching me, toying with me, but I'm already so flustered, it's as if my brain can't handle the terrifying predicament in which I've found myself.

My fear of being implicated in that man's murder is greater than my fear of my new stalker. If I am correct and the killer and my stalker are one and the same, he will soon be caught, investigated, and convicted. Then I can try my best to get back to a normal life. Hell, if all this mental turmoil ceases, maybe I can even go back to house hunting.

I don't want to get too ahead of myself because who knows how long this whole thing will last, but I can always begin to scout out new homes to keep my mind centered on something else... something that I love, something that brings me joy.

Sadly, that pleasure is tainted with the discovery at my last victim's house, but the odds of something like that happening again are impossible. They have to be impossible, right? Sure, I could still get caught in the near future, but I feel like the punishment for being found in a house you don't belong in would be far less harsh than the punishment I would receive for being in a house with a dead body, not reporting it, and concealing information that could lead to the arrest of the murderer.

I need to actively attempt to alter my mindset and focus on the more imminent danger of a stalker.

Looking at the big picture, being caught in someone's house, and only that.... Having done nothing to damage the property or steal anything, I feel like I would probably get off with a slap on the wrist.

That settles it. I won't enter any homes. Not yet. Instead, I'll concentrate on compiling a mental list of possible victims for me to target once I'm in the clear of this whole mess. It's near the end of the day, so now, as I pull into the coffee shop, I tell myself that the scouting can start tomorrow. That way, I'll have something to look forward to.

The anticipation alone lightens my mood almost instantly. I walk into the coffee shop with a jubilant sprint, which I'm sure is a clear improvement on my recently acquired somber gait. It's nowhere near back to the way I carry myself normally, but it's a halfway point, and a halfway point is not something I've thought possible these last few days, so I'll take it.

Kristi has noticed my diminished mood lately. She's been giving me some distance, and I appreciate her so much for that. Rather than peppering me with questions and assaulting me in an attempt to make me feel better, she has given me the space to figure things out on my own, even if that is not her intention.

I'm not sure if she realizes I'm going through something, but I truly hope she thinks I'm just trying to recover from a physical illness rather than what can more accurately be called a heady mental one.

"Hey," she says as I walk through the door. Her hair is tied up in a messy bun, glasses perched on the edge of her nose. The smell of coffee fills every inch of the space.

"Hey, had a good day here?"

"Sure did. Nothing to complain about," she sings in reply. *Must be nice.*

To try to get back to normal and capitalize on my slightly improved mood, I figured I'd come in and catch up with her. Before she has a chance to ask me any questions, I pose one to her.

"Man, I don't think we've gotten the chance to talk. What do you think about that whole crazy murder thing?"

"Oh my god. You're right. We both have been so busy just focusing on work, but there was a murder in town! How have we not talked about this yet?"

If only she knew.

"I feel like it's because of that stomach bug. It really took a lot out of me, and I really didn't start feeling better until today. That's how you know I don't feel well. When my nosy self isn't all up in everybody's business talking about a murder that basically happened next door."

"You ain't lying," she laughs. "Glad to hear you're feeling better, though."

"Not much to talk about, though, right? It's always just speculation until it isn't," I say with a shrug.

"Yeah. I haven't seen much actual news about anything. It's more like rumors around town and reading what people are commenting on the news posts." Then she looks up as if in thought.

"Actually, I haven't been on my phone for hours," she finishes before grabbing her phone out of the back of her jeans. As she brings the device to life, the light from her screen illuminates her face, allowing me to see her jaw drop as she lets out a gasp.

"They have a suspect in custody."

Chapter 15

The news of the suspect's capture fills me with relief. For once, I don't have to put on a show. My sense of relief doesn't have to be masked. It appears as if I'm happy because we've all avoided becoming the next victims and the town will now be safe, instead of the actual reason—relief that my stalker has been caught.

Things are finally looking up. I can almost feel the actual weight being lifted from my chest. I leave work that day with my shoulders straightened and my head held high.

You did nothing wrong.

My mantra, paired with the capture of the actual killer, brightens my mood immensely and only convinces me further that I can begin scouting and rummaging through houses again.

Oh, what a feeling! Almost a sense of freedom, a feeling that things are close to returning to how they used to be. I can start fresh, essentially. Hang out with friends more, go back to enjoying my job, and maybe if I'm lucky, I can find a new hobby that may surpass my current one.

I've just never really enjoyed the things most people do. Reading? No thanks, it just makes me tired. Arts and crafts? I can't even draw a straight line. Sports? Only if I want to end up in the hospital with broken bones.

I'm sure I can find something safer, but I just haven't found it yet.

I can't help but still wonder about the case. My curiosity knows no bounds. Now I can follow the case under the guise of a curious citizen rather than a madwoman who fears an impending false conviction for a crime she didn't commit.

Oh, maybe that's an option for a new hobby? Amateur sleuthing? I rule out the idea the moment it enters my head—too much extensive research and groundwork.

As soon as I pull into my driveway, I bring out my phone and begin searching for everything I can find online. It isn't much. My eyes remain glued to the screen as I walk to the door, which I unlock with the ease of any automatic task, akin to driving or singing the alphabet.

I plop down onto my white-cushioned sofa, the fluffy throw pillows catching me as I fall, and start to sink into my preferred spot, which has begun to remember the shape of my body and keep space for it.

I end up learning a little more than I already know about the case: They've finally taken Bartholomew Ledet into custody. He owns a local lawn care company—Ledet's Landscaping. In the time leading up to the murder, police were alerted to his presence at the home of the victim, Alan Hebert. Ledet was wanted for questioning but had evaded capture for a brief time following the murder. Due to the evidence found at the scene, the authorities don't believe the Southern Slasher is the killer. To preserve the integrity of the investigation, police aren't releasing many details to the public.

A notification pops up as I'm scrolling to find additional news stories, and when I see who's sent it, I release a small squeal of shock and delight. My ex, Lucas, has liked yet another picture of mine. I'm pretty sure this is the fourth week in a row he's done it. I'm not the type of person to post much, so he's intentionally going out of his way to like older pictures. Some aren't even selfies, just random everyday stuff. Now that I think of it, he seems to like them from oldest to newest. Wow, actually, now that I give it more consideration, maybe he's even doing it the same day once a week? What's he trying to do?

We dated for almost a year, about two years ago. I haven't dated anyone else seriously since then. I became obsessed with him, and usually, that scared guys away, but he gave back the same energy I was putting in and was just as obsessed with me. Over time, our involvement just became unhealthy. Not necessarily toxic, only it prevented us from accomplishing anything; all we did was pull each other down. We were young, and we should have had high aspirations and goals, but all we could focus on was each other.

When we first met, he was planning to become a tugboat captain, but we soon learned that we couldn't be apart that long. He gave up on his dream and found a menial nine-to-five job to keep him busy while I delivered iced coffees. Over time, I noticed a difference in his spirit, and I just knew that he'd grow to regret his decision of giving up his dream job just to spend time with me.

I worked up the courage to end the relationship. I loved him enough to break it off so that I couldn't interfere with the plans he'd made before he met me. Sure, we were obsessed with each other at the time, but that level of love wouldn't last forever. He would have grown to resent me and the choice he made because of me.

Breaking up with him was one of the hardest decisions I ever made. We were so in love. I tried to reason that I always fell deeply in love, obsessing over my partner every time, and I'd find someone else. So I broke it off with Lucas, and he didn't take it well.

He told me he was a grown man and could make his own decisions and didn't need me making them for him. He said I was worth the sacrifice, but I didn't budge on my decision. I'm pretty sure he was borderline stalking me for a while. I'd see his car at places that he knew I'd be. He'd park outside my house and stay there for hours. He'd also text me relentlessly, whether I replied or not.

Okay, so maybe he did stalk me. But he got the hint eventually. I stopped seeing him around. He stopped texting me.

I can't believe I didn't think of him sooner. I'd spent a lot of time trying to forget about him, though, so maybe that was why.

I'd always pushed him from my mind when I thought about him. After all this time, that still feels too frequent. I'm curious to know if he's become a tugboat captain—and also if my sacrifice has been rewarded, but I know how I am. I can't check in with him. I can't start looking into it, because then I won't stop. Then I'll be the stalker.

I've just gone on living, but when he throws himself into my life like this, it stirs feelings in me that I don't want to feel. It's so crazy to want something so badly while also wanting to push it away. It's difficult to know if I did the right thing and to maintain the willpower to compartmentalize it. Ironically, he taught me about the meaning of that word. See? It's hard enough to live without him in my life as it is. Although I don't even see him or talk to him, he pops into my mind.

I hate that after our years apart from each other, I still feel the same pull and the same amount of love for him. They should go away, right? Certain words make me think of him. So do specific songs that he'd tell me reminded him of me, or TV shows we talked about and watched together. I want so badly to reach out, but I vowed to him when I broke off our relationship that I was leaving him so he could be happy. He makes it hard to do.

I'm always unconsciously scanning the crowd for him—a man with an average build, glasses, and a goatee. I don't even realize I'm doing it until someone turns around, and the disappointment hits when I see it's not him.

Even now, I still get lost in memories and thoughts of him, and all he did was like a post of mine! I shake my head as though doing so will ease his hold on my mind.

A new thought interrupts my nostalgia. I should call Bianca now that the suspect's name has been made public. Not necessarily to find out anything more, just to reassure her and let her know I'm serious about rekindling our friendship.

"Hey, Queen," she says jokingly when she answers the phone.

A callback to when I was miraculously nominated for homecoming court, even though I never had a chance at winning.

"Very funny. What are you up to?"

"Just working..." she says, her voice trailing off, possibly trying to indicate that she can't talk too much or for too long.

"Ahhh, this late?" I say, looking at the clock—the one on the wall this time. I have to make sure it stays upright. Yep, she'd usually be off by now.

"As you can imagine, it's a little crazy around here."

"Oh yeah, I saw that. Well, I felt like calling to let you know I was thinking about you."

"Oh, that's so sweet. But I've got to be honest with you; I'm not looking for anything serious. I'm almost a married woman, you know?" she says, messing with me once again.

"Hardy-har. Okay, well, I don't want to bother you too much at work. I just wanted to tell you that you're a star employee and they're lucky to have you."

She snorts in reply.

"Yeah, well, tell my boss, would ya? Oops, hold on a sec."

I hear what I think is her putting her phone down, followed by a muffled conversation. A few minutes pass before I hear her voice over the phone again.

"Sorry," she says before dropping her voice to a whisper. "That was the guy's lawyer."

She doesn't have to say which guy. I know exactly who she's talking about. Bartholomew Ledet.

"Oh yeah, just signing out?" I inquire, fishing for more information.

"Yeah, he said something about delivering a message when he left here. Pursuit of justice and all that. These lawyers can be so full of themselves."

I can almost hear her eyes rolling over the phone.

"Well, all right. Try not to work too hard. Talk to you later."

We exchange goodbyes and hang up our phones. My stomach growls, which I interpret as a good sign. Perhaps my hunger is recovering.

Now comes an easy decision. One of the easiest I've had to make in days. Not what to do or what to think but what to eat?

Chapter 16

When I get back home from picking up supper, the night has settled in and cast everything in shadows, especially my front porch. I forgot to turn on my porch light before I left. I could keep it on all the time, but I don't usually get home after dark, so it stays off.

It's probably just the way everything has been going for me in general lately, but coming home tonight doesn't feel welcoming. It feels eerie, the way my house is awaiting me silently in the dark. The familiar rising and falling chirping of the cicadas should aid in diminishing the unsettling feeling, but it doesn't.

I glance next door quickly when I see movement from the corner of my eye, but as I focus on the darkness, I spot nothing out of the ordinary.

As I approach my front door, the ominous sensation settles deeper. There's another note on the door.

How is that possible? Once again, I'm frozen in place outside my door as my thoughts race uncontrollably. Why must my mind be a constant war zone?

The paper appears to be the same size as last time, about half as big as my hand, and looks darker than most paper too. The last note was on an unusual kind of paper—thicker, with a blue tinge to it. Even in the shadows, I can tell that this note looks almost identical to the last one. It can't be. He's in custody. Was this note here earlier and I just never noticed it? That's possible, maybe, but how could I walk by it so many times and only see it now? And in the dark at that.

Suddenly, Bianca's words from our phone call come back to me.

Something about delivering a message when he left here.

No, surely he wouldn't have asked his lawyer to leave a note. Can a lawyer do this? Isn't that kind of juvenile? Wouldn't they just give my name to the police? Wouldn't that make the most sense if they're trying to do what I think they are? If they want to cast doubt on Bartholomew's guilt?

I can see how they might try to claim that if he's guilty of being in the wrong place at the wrong time, then so am I.

The mosquitoes biting incessantly at my exposed skin finally pull me from thought and convince me to go inside. I grab the note and begin to let myself in, my legs already itching from the flying predators.

"Hey."

The sudden, unexpected deep voice that thunders through the quiet shocks me so much that I almost drop everything as I turn around defensively.

My neighbor, Eric, is standing in the shadows that border our two homes. He rarely speaks to me, but I've never taken offense to it or judged him. He's a few years older than me, and he's always struck me as an introvert, so we don't speak often.

His eerie hello and recent criminal conviction, paired with the ominous note clutched in my hands, have me shaking uncontrollably.

"Um, hey," I reply curiously before continuing, "Did you see who left this note?"

I ask him, and although I'm not sure if he can perceive it, I hear the desperation in my voice.

"N-No," he stutters, which isn't unusual for him based on our previous encounters. "I was just heading back inside from taking out the trash when I saw you get home. With a killer on the loose, I didn't want to spook you. I thought letting you know I was here and that I wasn't some stranger would ease your mind."

Well, it didn't work. That's what I think, at least.

"Thanks, that's sweet of you. You haven't seen anything out of the ordinary or anyone strange around, have you?"

"Nah, I haven't."

"Okay, well, thanks. Let me know if you do?"

"Sure thing," he mumbles before averting his gaze, turning his back to me, and walking home.

I stand there for a moment, pondering our awkward encounter, before I finally push my door open and hurry into the safety of my house.

Once inside, my skin feels as if insects are crawling all over it, but as I look down, I see the mosquitoes are gone, and the sensation is just my nerves settling in to put me on edge. Well, I can't put this off any longer, and with a hand on each side of the paper, I pull it up into my line of sight.

I saw you there.

Oh man. This has to be from good ol' Bart himself. It must be from him and delivered by his lawyer, even though that seems so juvenile and outside the typical protocol. Why not just rat me out to the police? Unless he did already, and this is just a warning?

God. Just when things are looking up, I get stuck in my head again with questions, my body shaking in fear.

Yes, he saw what I did, and while breaking and entering is a much lesser charge than murder, he can cast blame on me to shed doubt on him. That's got to be his intention. Ugh. I must have shown up just after he murdered that guy. That was why I didn't smell the blood at first.

This is crazy. You can't make this stuff up. I literally begin to pull strands of my hair at the base in an attempt to ease the tension building in my skull. I must try to ease my anxiety.

I'm a good person. I shouldn't have to feel like this as often and as severely as I do.

You did nothing wrong. You did nothing wrong.

"You didn't. You tell the police that," I say aloud.

"He'll lie to the police," I reply.

Now I know I'm starting to lose it; I'm talking to myself. That's not normal, although maybe I can think better like this. Throw ideas back and forth and try to focus on one thought at a time by verbalizing each one as it arrives.

"Okay. If both of us were there and both of us claim to be innocent, then each of us can cast reasonable doubt on the other. They can't convict both of us for the same crime, so maybe they have to let both of us go?

"I don't know. Has anything like that happened before? Surely it has. But you're right. *I'm* right. If he claims that I was there and could be the murderer, I can very well say the same thing about him," I reason with myself.

Forcefully, I push out a breath to try to calm my nerves. As I do, my phone vibrates in my pocket.

Oh no. Is it Bianca warning me that the police are on their

way? Would she warn me? We are friends, after all. Should I run? Could I run? I have nowhere to go. What little family I have left lives here, so there's no fleeing out of state. I've been here in Houma my whole life, so I don't have any friends outside of Louisiana. I don't have enough money to support myself, and surely the authorities will make it so I can't access the funds I do have.

Once again, I tell myself, *I am not guilty! I shouldn't have to run!*

I pull my phone from my pocket, and the screen comes to life with a text notification from Lucas. Lucas?

I can't help but experience this confusing mix of feelings every time that he reminds me of his existence, whether it's by a post from him or when he likes my pictures, but a text? He hasn't texted me in what feels like forever. Just like always, though, I feel a surge of elation and lust; at the same time, I feel the pressure of sacrifice and loss. A text is far different from a like or a shared post. No, a text is intentional and direct.

No time to act nonchalant and put off reading it to pretend I've got better things to do. Instead, curiosity eats at me. Well, I always have time for my hypothetical scenarios....

Maybe he finally has his captain's license and wants to get back together, and instead of driving tugboats, he's driving for rich people who will let me live with him on a yacht while he drives them around the world? Is *drive* the right word? Anyway, that would be a dream come true but very unlikely.

Maybe he's texting me to tell me that he's almost done with his schooling and about to start working, but he wants to try again and will suggest that we both try to be less obsessed with one another?

Or maybe it's a random text with a random excuse to talk to

me in the hopes that I'll respond although our situation hasn't changed? I feel like any of these outcomes are possible, and my body is almost vibrating with excitement to read what he has to say.

Shaking, I unlock my phone and open the text.

Loo-Kiss: *What ya been up to, Rosy?*

Man, I forgot he used to call me that. Nosy Rosy but Rosy for short. I can't wipe the smile off my face. I honestly can't help but feel pure happiness reading his text. I allow myself the time to soak in the feeling so I can try to relax my body and ease my nerves. Finally, my body stops shaking, and I need to decide what to do. I really shouldn't reply, because I can lose myself easily in conversation with him, and it might be nearly impossible to halt the trajectory of intimacy between us. I'll end up right where I spent all this time trying to avoid being.

Wait a minute. He called me Rosy. He would only call me that when I was being nosy or overtly curious about something. Is it possible that he knows about what I'm going through? Is that the reason he's been liking my posts out of nowhere? The timeline matches, and he's been very insistent about his intentions. Almost like Morse code. One like, once a week, for weeks now, almost always on the same day...

Oh my god. What if he's the one stalking me? What if he's the one leaving the notes?

Chapter 17

I decided not to text Lucas back last night. It was all just too much, and I had to work through some things. I don't know who to trust these days. Finding that body has my mind in shambles.

Now here I am at work, going through the motions, putting on a show for those around me, all while struggling with myself internally.

I never noticed until I started to experience all this trauma, but I'm so isolated. That never bothered me before. Living by myself and working most of the day on my own was fine. I was happy getting to be myself and do my own thing without others around to judge or demand more from me. I feel so lonely now. I've backed myself into a corner.

That's why it's easy for me to make the decision that I'm going to make. I'll text Lucas that I want to catch up with him. I have no idea what his intentions are, but I've got to find out. I don't want him to know that I suspect he's been stalking me. I feel as if I act naïve and helpless, I'll get a lot more information from him and be able to analyze his interactions without making him suspicious that I'm doing it.

Currently, I'm waiting to pick up my next round of iced coffees. Before I lose my cool, I grab my phone from the cupholder. I pull up the text from last night, but I freeze there because I don't know how to word my response. I want Lucas to know I'm excited to hear from him, but it won't seem that way since I've taken so long to reply.

I rack my brain for excuses, but I think the best thing to do is not acknowledge the delay at all.

Zoey: *Hey! It's been a minute, hmm? Free to catch up in person sometime soon?*

I send the message quickly and then lock the phone and place it back in the cupholder. Heat spreads quickly across my body. The air from the AC is coating my skin with a nice breeze, rustling the baby hairs that frame my face, but it's not enough. I reach forward and put the fan on high, causing the cool air to jet toward me. I have a feeling the heat that I'm experiencing isn't from the outside temperature. No, it's from the reality of what I've just done. What I've just re-kindled. It's from the anticipation of his reply.

I grab my phone again and send Kaci and Sierra a random GIF image just to let them know that I'm thinking of them.

It's time to get my next round of orders, so I put my SUV into drive and ease my way onto the road and back to the store.

As I pull up to the store, I realize I didn't even have the radio on. I've just been sitting in silence all morning, my thoughts swarming, with nothing to focus on except my impending doom.

Suddenly my phone chimes, and I grab it quickly and see that Lucas has replied. I rush to open his text.

Loo-Kiss: *Sure thing. My place or yours?*

Whoa, that's very presumptuous. Now I need even more to know what's going on in his head. I really should play it safe and insist on meeting in public, but I don't want him to suspect I'm onto him. My house is safer, since he'll be on my home turf.

Zoey: *Meet me at my house tonight, say 7?*

Loo-Kiss: *It's a date.*

Wow, how can I feel two opposite emotions simultaneously? Giddiness and trepidation?

* * *

I'm biting my nails. Jesus, I haven't done that since high school! I'm nervous for a ridiculous number of reasons. The possibility of false imprisonment for murder. A stalker ex-boyfriend. Spiraling mental health. An omnipresent sense of danger. Things that are most definitely not normal for a young woman such as me.

Being stalked by Lucas is an unusual predicament to be in. I have nothing to hide from him, and I'll always love him. It's interesting that I'm not as alarmed as I should be. What I'm more worried about is whether he saw me that day or if it's just a big coincidence. Is he the one leaving me the notes, or is it Bartholomew, or even someone else? Ugh, the agony.

I've dolled myself up a bit for tonight. I applied a thin layer of makeup, sprayed a light floral perfume that I hadn't used in ages, wore some clothes that fit better (now that I've lost my usual appetite and have replaced eating with anxiety-riddled thoughts), and I even shaved my legs, because why not.

Is it crazy to go from accusing your ex of stalking you and planning to interrogate him under the guise of rekindling a romance to focusing more on the romance part? I guess it depends on whether I think he's guilty or not. That has yet to be determined. I can't help but be excited to see him. I also can't help but want to impress him.

A loud knock on the door interrupts my thoughts, and I nervously wipe my hands down the sides of my body, flattening my tight T-shirt dress and drying my sweaty hands simultaneously. The aroma of my perfume permeates the air, though, so I think that should coat any underlying stench of nervous sweat.

I walk slowly to the door, partly in fear, despite how eager I am to see Lucas. I don't have to fake the smile on my face as I open the door to find Lucas there. Man, I've missed him. He stands there frozen, smiling as he takes me in, just as my gaze analyzes everything about him.

His short brown hair waves slightly in the light breeze, his green eyes are piercing, and the stubble on his chin is in the midst of transitioning to a thick, dark brown beard. I swoon and sigh internally. I love when he grows out his beard.

I can no longer resist the urge to hug him. I slide my arms under his just as he raises them and wraps them around my shoulders. He's a little taller than me, and we fit together perfectly as we embrace. I can't help but squeeze him, and he squeezes me back with the same ferocity. His familiar scent surrounds me—sandalwood. I hold on to him probably longer than I should, but I find so much comfort and peace in his embrace, which is so invigorating after all the unusual goings-on in my life. I stiffen slightly at that thought, hoping he can't sense it. He could be involved, and although it's hard to think of it that way, he may very well be a contributing factor to my constant paranoia.

I pull away from his embrace, gesture for him to enter, and close the door behind him.

"Long time no see," I tell him as he sits on the sofa.

I join him there, not even bothering to offer him a drink. I'm too anxious to talk to him to even ask him if he wants a glass of water. As I sit on the opposite side of the same sofa, I lift my leg, which I tuck underneath me while ensuring my dress doesn't ride up, and position myself to face him slightly rather than directly.

The magnetism he has is amazing; I can almost feel his pull, beckoning me to slide toward him. The urge to curl into the underside of his arm is almost impossible to fight. I have to be polite and stay where I am. We're not together anymore, and it's completely inappropriate. I don't even know if he has a girlfriend. He's also here for me to try to determine if he's stalking me. It's baffling that despite that, I'm more excited than I am concerned.

"Yeah, it's been a minute. I'm glad you texted me back. I wasn't sure you would."

I blanch. I'm completely unprepared for this conversation. Well, I had a plan, but now that I see him here in person, the whole thing has gone out the window. How can this kind soul be stalking me? Honestly, if he is, I'm not even scared.

Why am I justifying stalking?

"How could I not?" I admit before the silence between us can go on too long.

He smiles at me, causing me to smile back, and I blush as a result. I want to appear bashful and look away, but I can't take my eyes off him.

"I was elated to hear from you," I add.

"So we're just going to jump into the big-word competition like nothing?" he asks me, and I laugh in response.

He always loved it when I used what he would refer to as my 75-cent words, so much so that he started cataloging random "big words" to throw at me in response for when I would use one.

"Oh, come on, 'elate' isn't too crazy," I say as I bend my head and inch toward him slowly. The urge to nudge him and graze his skin overpowers any other feeling in this moment, and I still leave space between us, although it's difficult.

"I dare say 'incongruent,' Zoey," he says, lifting his chin to the air, feigning arrogance.

I laugh wholeheartedly. I've missed the banter between us. Just like that, I remember how good he is at making me laugh, even if the joke is at his expense.

"You most definitely used that one incorrectly," I say with a snort.

"Ah, the snort! I missed that snort of yours."

"Said no one ever!" I squeal.

We've been separated for years, not acknowledging one another, now only reconnected by unsavory life events, and I still feel the irresistible hold he has on me. Unable to be apart from him a second longer, I lunge to his side of the couch and snuggle into his side, saying nothing.

I don't have to either. He wraps an arm around me and holds me to him as I savor his smell, the touch of his skin, and the weight of his presence. I completely allow myself a bit of light and joy for a moment.

After a few minutes of silence, I look up at him and see him smiling down.

"I missed you, Lucas."

"Same, Zoey. Still delivering coffees?"

"Yes. I love it. It barely pays the bills, but I'll always have that money on the side from that lawsuit."

I don't like to talk about how I lost my dad, and I don't have to tell Lucas because he knows. An offshore accident killed him and a few other workers, which resulted in a lawsuit that awarded money to all the families involved.

It was hard to lose him when I did, shortly after high school, knowing he'd never be able to walk me down the aisle. Nothing good ever comes with the loss of a loved one. So much happened that was out of my control, though, and I couldn't grieve like I would have liked. Since I couldn't say goodbye to him, I wanted to go through his belongings and keep important mementos. Unfortunately, my mom couldn't bear to be reminded of him, and she threw almost all of his things away. The combination of not only losing him unexpectedly but also being unable to sort through his things is something from which I don't think I've ever truly recovered. Sadly, I lost her, too, not very long ago, and consequently inherited my parents' meager wealth.

"I'm happy doing what I do, though, and I take pride in that because not many people can truthfully say that they love their job," I tell him, even though I don't have to. He knows. Lucas was a part of my life. He still knows me so well.

"What about you?" I ask.

Something I've been dying to know. Ready to learn whether my sacrifice paid off. Asking a question to which I know the answer will determine the whole trajectory of our relationship.

He looks down at his chest, seeming almost ashamed.

"Well, I started on the boats and learned the ropes to try to become a captain, but I just wasn't catching on like I hoped. It was far more laborious than I imagined. I know that after all the hard work, I would have had a nice gig and a good-paying one at that, but I couldn't tough it out. I hate to say it like that, but it's true. Not only was it a lot of work, but I kept thinking about the responsibility of being a captain. Being held accountable for all the men working for me, for the cargo, and for their safety. If anything goes wrong, the captain's the fall guy."

"Wow, yeah, I guess I never thought of it like that."

"Yeah, so I left well enough alone and gave up the boat life altogether. I got a job with a heating-and-AC company instead."

With his response, the thoughts pulse through my head:

Because of me, he tried.

We can be together again.

He hasn't been on a boat for weeks at a time.

He could be the one watching me and leaving cryptic notes.

He could very well be stalking me.

Chapter 18

Once I realized that Lucas could have been the one leaving the notes, I tried to put on a brave face and ignore the ominous feeling in the pit of my stomach until he left. I think the conflict was evident on my face, though, because after a few hours, he said I looked distracted and that he would come by another time.

I was relieved, but I was also afraid that I'd made my suspicions of him too obvious and my actions would clue him in that he'd been found out. But I don't think they did. He looked genuinely concerned for me, even kissing me on the head as I walked him to the door last night.

The old me, the stable and undeterred version of me, would be bouncing off the walls with excitement at the possibility of picking things back up with him. Not anymore. These days, I know too much, suspect too much, and have a heavy burden on my shoulders. Oddly enough, I need to pretend to be the old version of myself, since no one can really understand what I'm going through.

If it is the worst-case scenario and he's stalking me... I don't know what to do. It's inappropriate, and he may have seen me doing highly illegal things. He may even think I'm a murderer. At this point, I feel like all I can do is act unaware and proceed with encouraging this relationship in the hopes of learning more and discovering that poor Lucas is innocent.

What would the old me do right now?

When I think of it like that, well, I know the answer immediately. I should be gushing about this to the girls. So I scoop up my phone from next to me on the couch, where the device has been since I got home from work an hour ago.

I put on a brave face before initiating a video call with Bianca. This "relationship" is still fresh, so there's no need to go involving Kaci and Sierra just yet, lest they get mad and lecture me. They'll surely end up begging me not to start ghosting them again now that I may have a boyfriend.

Whoa, I'm getting ahead of myself.

Bianca picks up after a few rings, and I soon see her puffy cheeks and blond hair, the latter of which has been thrown into a messy bun atop her head.

"Gosh, I needed to see your beautiful face!" she says, not even bothering to begin with a hello.

"I know you did. That's why this is a video and not a text," I joke.

"But really, I can't tell if it's the video quality or not, but you look tired!"

Uh-oh. My restless nights must be starting to show. I look at the spot on the phone that shows my face, and yep, I look exhausted. Anybody could tell that I hadn't been sleeping.

"It's just a filter," I laugh, hoping she won't pry further.

"Yeah, okay. To what do I owe the pleasure?"

"Wellll, guess who came to visit me last night?" I ask, hiking up one eyebrow, curious if she'll guess.

She furrows her brow in concentration before she says, "Who?"

"What? No guess?" I ask softly.

"I'm too curious to guess! I want to *know*!"

"Okay, okay. Lucas," I say, adding nothing more, because I truly don't know how she'll feel about it.

"Lucas, Lucas? *The* Lucas? What? How? Why? Tell me all the things!" she says, shaking her phone, causing her image to distort briefly before she stills the device enough for it to refocus.

"He's been liking my posts over the past few weeks. He texted me the other day, and I just decided, why not catch up?" I say with a shrug.

"I mean, I guess you're right. It's not like he did anything bad to you. He's really always been so darn nice."

"Yeah. I wanted to see how he's been, and guess what? He basically couldn't be a boat captain, so he's got a whole new job and outlook on life."

I pause, waiting for her to put what she knows and what she's learning together so that she can form her own opinions. I want to hear what she has to say, not what she may think I want to hear.

"Wow, y'all will be back together in no time. This could be good! He could be a whole husband!" she says excitedly.

I giggle and say, "A whole husband is how they come nowadays, I think." I cannot help a blush from spreading across my face. Then I add, "I mean, yeah, this could really turn into something. Before you say anything... I'm going to get better at controlling my emotions."

She rolls her eyes at me.

"I'm serious. I know that I get too obsessive and cut y'all out. It's wrong, and I'm not doing it. Record this! I vow not to dedicate all my free time to him."

Which is true, because can I even trust him?

"Oh, so that's why you look so tired! It all makes sense now. You were doing something else instead of sleeping!" she squeals as she finishes her sentence.

I palm my forehead.

"No! I'm going to take it slow. I *am* taking it slow. I am not diving in headfirst. I will not get attached and exclude myself from things with y'all," I say, trying to convince her.

I don't need to convince myself, just her. I think this small wrench in the gears can ease my typical obsessive tendencies toward non-platonic relationships. Lucas could be a stalker, after all. I like him, but I also like my privacy and for people to respect boundaries.

I'm a hypocrite, I know.

Bianca beams at me from the phone.

"Whatttt?" I say, groaning.

"I'm just so proud of you. You're growing up," she says as she pretends to wipe away a nonexistent tear.

Just as I'm about to confirm her statement, acknowledge that I am indeed "growing up," I notice something—and stiffen at the sight.

I look back at the phone screen to see if Bianca has also noticed, and I can tell she has sensed the immediate change in my demeanor, since her smile has morphed to a look of confusion.

"What?" she asks.

"Um, nothing. I thought maybe I had heard someone at the door. Did you hear that?" I lie, hoping that she can't detect my dishonesty, although my face still appears haunted.

"No, but if so, you're fine. Could just be a delivery," she rationalizes.

I pretend to be relieved and effortfully ease the tension from my body so that she won't worry about me more.

"You're probably right. Or it could be Eric. He spoke to me yesterday! Crazy how it just seems like no one knocks on doors these days, at least not like they used to."

I seem to have done a good job at disarming her, since her smile comes back, and she launches into a story about how her aunt literally threw herself on the floor when someone knocked on the door while she was visiting her aunt's house one weekend.

"Okay, so it's not just me," I say, faking a smile.

"Well, let me go see what they dropped off. Talk to you soon?" I ask her.

"Guaranteed! New boyfriend or not! Or is it *new-old* boyfriend or not?" she teases.

"Oh my gosh, yes! You have my word. Bye!" I say as I press the red end-call button.

I make sure Bianca's face is no longer visible as I look back up and stare at what shocked me into a stupor in the first place.

I stare now at my entertainment center. Usually, my TV sits in the middle, while fake chrysanthemums rest in a cat-shaped vase on the left, and a framed photograph of my parents and me at my high school graduation rests on the right.

Currently, they've switched places. The picture is now off to the left, while the flowers decorate the right.

Chapter 19

Someone's watching me.

They've been in my house. They know what I do and what I have done, and they're giving it back to me tenfold. I can't say I don't deserve this, but that doesn't make it any less unsettling.

I know that I could have played it off and shown Bianca, asking if she remembered how the arrangement was the last time she was over, but I was afraid doing that would make me look crazy. The instant I saw it, I was shocked. I can't help feeling like this change is easier to explain than the clock's upside-down position, though. But jeez, put both of those together and something is not making sense.

Well, now I know how people feel when I do it to them. I always wonder if they notice the things I've moved—if they blow off the inconsistency, accuse a loved one, or simply stare in confusion. For me, I just stare. I can't easily explain this away by accusing a sibling or a spouse, because it's only me here. The unexpected discovery leaves my mouth instantly dry.

Except last night, it wasn't just me. Lucas was here. I can still smell his scent, which lingers on the sofa, just barely.

No, no, no. He wouldn't have, would he?

I did go to the bathroom at one point. Did he move my things around while I was out of the living room? I try to imagine what it looked like last night, but I was so enthralled by him that I didn't notice anything else.

But what about the clock? Did he do that too? How did he get in? Maybe I should invest in one of those video doorbell cameras. You'd think I would have one, since I, of all people, target homes that don't have them.

Stupid, stupid, stupid.

I so wanted to believe Lucas was innocent and all this was merely a coincidence. However, I can't deny this. It's tangible, not my imagination or speculation. The evidence is right there, and the odds are not in his favor.

What satisfaction does he get from doing this to me? Does he even want to make things work with me, or is he just seeking to torment me? I truly don't understand his endgame, and I find that so unsettling.

It can't be. Maybe I did it when I cleaned one day, not noticing that I put the objects down in the opposites of their usual positions after I completed dusting. I zone out sometimes, so that could be a plausible explanation.

I definitely can't ask Bianca if she remembers what my entertainment center looked like, since she'll most definitely accuse me of losing my mind. Which, frankly, I basically am, but I don't want people to notice.

I can hear it now.

"Oh, hey, Bianca? Do you remember my entertainment center last week? Were the flowers to the left of the TV, or to the right? Just so I know that you're not guessing, tell me what kind of flowers they were and what picture is in the frame."

Yep, not doing that. I'll definitely either clue her in to my paranoia or, worse, scare her away for good.

Wait, Bianca knows where I keep the spare key to my house.

Could she be... no. Pushing that thought from my head as quickly as the idea appeared.

I also can't call the police; they won't take me seriously because nothing has been stolen and I have no proof of anyone breaking into my home. Not to mention that I'm trying to stay out of their way, not walk right into it.

I check the locks on my doors and windows, ensuring that they're fastened, and pour myself a glass of water to help me swallow some allergy medicine. The pill's chalky taste is slightly dulled with the introduction of the cold water. I know the medicine shouldn't be taken solely to induce drowsiness, but I hope it'll do exactly that. Enough for me to get some semblance of sleep.

Once in my room, I lie down in bed and start researching affordable cameras online. I don't need anything fancy. Just something cheap with a simple setup that I can put inside my house to catch anyone who might be moving my stuff around under my nose. I basically need a baby monitor that records, maybe something like a nanny cam.

I scroll for a solid hour, studying product descriptions, comparing prices, reading reviews, and adding items to my cart as I go. Eventually, once I have a few choices, I narrow them down to find the most cost-effective one that can send a recording to my phone. I should have done this a long time ago.

You'd think purchasing the camera would bring me some peace of mind and afford me a relatively peaceful send-off to slumber, but just like most nights as of late, I lie there unable to sleep. I squeeze my eyes shut and shift into my ideal sleeping position—lying on my right side, with my lower leg stretched out and my top leg pulled up toward my chest. I try to clear my head, but it's impossible.

Every night, it's something different, but after today's events, what I begin to wonder, above all, is, *who left the notes?*

As I think about it, they couldn't possibly be from Bartholomew's lawyer. Right? If they were, I'd think the cops would call me in for questioning. Gosh, what if that happens? What if the police come for me? Can I keep my cool and evade suspicion?

I can feign ignorance and affirm my innocence. I can't let them intimidate me or do anything that would lead them to suspect me or give credence to Bartholomew's accusations. Worse yet, the police may have evidence to put me behind bars. There's no end to the stories I can imagine about the women I'd encounter in a place like prison.

If the notes are from Lucas, well, that sucks because I don't know what he thinks of me and how we could proceed. If the notes are from Bartholomew, the police can come to arrest me at any time. If the notes are from someone else and the real killer is still out there, I could be his next victim.

Oh great. Here I am trying to fall asleep, and all I can do is create additional, quite plausible, frightful scenarios.

The speculative and creative stories I conceive are entertaining when the main characters are strangers that I don't know. But now that these narratives are swarming with me at the forefront, they're insurmountable.

Chapter 20

The killer could come after me.

I thought prison would be bad, but what if the murderer is involved somehow and now has their sights set on me? I could die! My friends would be devastated—getting me back in their lives only for me to be ripped out of them.

Kristi would be screwed, and her business could suffer.

Lucas, sweet Lucas. We could never be. Again, another possible future afforded to me only to be taken away. I sacrificed our relationship and accepted that we couldn't be together, and just when that seemed like it was about to change...

Wait! If the real killer is leaving the creepy notes, then that means Lucas isn't stalking me! The joy and relief wash through me like a flood but are soon stopped by a dam—the dam of my death. If Lucas isn't the stalker, then the source of the notes wishes me either dead or incarcerated. No happily ever after for me.

What will the headlines say? "Local Woman Convicted Murderer"? "Local Woman Slain in Home by Unidentified Killer"? "Terrebonne Resident Most Recent Victim of the Southern Slasher"?

By now, is there any way for me to escape this whole thing?

Come on, I'm good at making up stories, so let's do one with a happy ending.

No one saw me at the house, so I'm overreacting. The notes are actually from a guy down the street who thinks I'm pretty, but he is socially awkward and going about it the wrong way. He tells me one day, and I laugh, letting him down politely, telling him that I'm in a beautiful relationship with Lucas. Sure, I saw a dead body, but the shock of that will diminish over time. I'll start going to therapy, and my therapist will reassure me of my innocence. I'll keep my job, and at the end of a great workday, I'll come home to my future husband. I'll spend time with my friends on the weekends, and everything will be fine. Yes, that's plausible. That's the future I want. That's the future I need.

Easy to say and easy to make up but not guaranteed to happen like that. I could say that easily about all my negative thoughts, but that's not how anxiety works, apparently.

I pull up to work, and as I walk in, Kristi offers me a kind smile.

"Ready to deliver some sunshine?"

"Little Miss Sunshine at your service," I say with a bow.

"Here ya go, Sunshine," she says as she pushes my mystery drink of the day toward me.

"Hmmmm," I ponder, my finger on my chin as I observe the color of the coffee and rack my brain. We offer so many flavors, and this one could be almost anything.

"Pistachio cream?" I ask her, lifting one eyebrow in inquisition.

"Nope! Gotcha. Crème brûlée," she says as she points at the cup with her right hand.

"Yum! One of my favorite perks of the job!"

"Oh yeah? What exactly are the other perks?"

"Listening to music all day, performing solo karaoke concerts in my car, and limited interaction with the public, all while getting paid. Best. Job. Ever."

I surprise myself with how quickly I can switch from *woe is me* mode to *everything's fine* mode.

She laughs at my wonderfully crafted bullet points, and soon enough, I'm alone in my car again, ready to start another day.

As I leave the shop, I decide that I'll try to be more observant today. Of course, I'm always observant but never about the things about which I *should* be.

I need to start paying attention to any possible patterns so I can see if anyone is watching me, stalking me, or planning to kill me. I've got to switch gears. I need to focus on being the predator instead of the prey.

Instead of narrowing my sights, I'm going to broaden them. I analyze every car that I pass and any identifying characteristics it has: bumper stickers, damage, license plate frames. That way, I'll know if I spot the same car again as the day continues.

I look at every person and pay attention, cataloging everything from their face to where I saw them, down to the clothes they wear. I'm sure if I do this long enough, I can determine if someone's watching me. Stalking me. I might even be lucky enough to find out who they are.

Oh, I can even detour as the days go by, interrupting my usual routine, which may make it easier for me to catch them. Look at me. Maybe I should be an undercover cop or something. I may have missed my true calling.

At first, it's kind of boring to make myself remember all the cars I see and the people I encounter, but as the day goes on, I realize I kind of already know everything. My route's typically the same, and I go to the same places on the same days. Without even having to try, I can predict what I'll find when I enter certain neighborhoods. The same driveways that are usually empty are still empty. The joggers I've seen before are still jogging at the same time and place as they usually do.

Even the woman who I saw walking her Pomeranian weeks ago still typically does so on the same route, and I usually see her on the same day around the same area. Of course, that's not always exact. Some people get sick, go on vacation, or have a life event that changes their schedule. For the most part, though, things are always the same.

I look for the woman and her Pomeranian today as I approach the stop sign. I also glance at the clock to confirm I'm passing at the time I usually do, and sure enough, like clockwork, the time is almost exactly what it's been every other time I've stopped to notice.

However, today's different, since she is not here with the dog, but as I look off into the distance, I do notice a dreary sky. She might have expected it to rain and didn't want to get caught in the weather, choosing instead to let the dog out quickly around the house.

It's amazing to me that I can visualize her face so vividly and that I even know she has a small scar above her left eye. I know that her frizzy blond hair will probably be held up on the back of her head with a claw clip. I also know that she prefers to wear capri leggings more than she does shorts or pants, based on what I usually see her in. I know her routine for this time of day on this day of the week, but I don't even know her name or any other details about her.

Identifying anything that stands out may be easier than I've thought. Even now I'm noticing this woman's absence, so let's hope I can spot other things to help me determine if anybody's watching me.

Chapter 21

I think I'm in the clear—well, for the most part. It's been days since I've received the ominous note on my doorstep, and the police haven't come to call yet.

I don't know how to feel about that. I'm the perfect scapegoat, or at least Bartholomew's key to getting out of jail. If his defense team plays their cards right, at least. They must not know about me after all. Unless... they're keeping the knowledge of my presence at the scene of the crime in their back pocket.

Bianca's been worried about me. Even though we are closer than we've been in months, she must be able to tell I'm not myself. She's constantly texting me, asking what I'm up to and checking in on me without actually coming out and saying, "How are you doing?"

I don't mind the attention, though. It's nice to have her back in my life and always within reach. I'd like to say her availability keeps my mind off of things, and sometimes it truly does. Sometimes I can even pretend that nothing life-altering is even happening.

Lucas and I have been texting, but I think he can sense my hesitation and is giving me the space I need. It's refreshing to learn that he's grown, as have I, in the time since we've been apart. It appears as if we are no longer the self-centered, love-obsessed pair we once were. We're more grounded now.

I don't even check the news or scroll social media because I prefer to push the whole subject from my mind. Soon, the public will forget about this circus, and the media will find something else to report on. It's a big deal for our small town now, but eventually, the crime will fade from the news and from people's minds. It'll be a little harder for me to forget because of my involvement, but I hope I'll find a way later to go days without thinking of it, and when I do, I'll be able to finally dispel the negative thoughts.

Just then, a knock at my door causes me to freeze. Goose bumps pepper my flesh. They're here. They've finally come for me. My freedoms, my job, my friends, my recently rekindled relationship with Lucas... They'll all be gone as soon as I answer that door.

I look down at what I'm wearing and determine I'm dressed sufficiently for a mug shot, in a white T-shirt and pair of jean shorts.

As I smooth down my shirt to try to straighten out some wrinkles, I stand up from the sofa. My legs are shaking so much that I have to use my arms to help lift me to my feet. Fear and worry vibrate through me, and as if beckoned, another knock lands heavily on my front door, frightening me and making me jump.

No use in postponing the inevitable. If they've found me like this, they have to know something, and trying to run out the back door would only make me more suspect.

"Coming," I yell, with an evident quiver in my voice as I walk toward the door so that they don't break it down.

I drag my feet along the floor, unable to lift them fully. My mind is telling my body there's no need to rush to my demise.

As my hand grasps the cold knob, I think of how this is the last time I'll open the door for a long while. Who will ensure my bills are paid? Who will keep my home clean and safe from vandals while I'm gone? Can I even keep this house while in prison?

I turn the knob slowly, squeezing my eyes shut, more in fear than to shield them from the sun's rays as they intrude on my privacy. Before I can open my eyes, arms wrap around me.

Jesus, I'm opening the door willingly and without a weapon! Are they truly going to tackle me?

Instead, the arms brace around my lower back, pulling me closer, and I open my eyes to see Bianca's blond hair just as I smell her all-too-familiar scent of patchouli.

Oh my god. It's just Bianca! But why is she here, and why hasn't she texted me and told me she was coming? Wait, actually, now that I think about it, my phone may be dead. It hasn't been charging well, and I think I've used up what little battery I had left. I figured it would last longer, since I hadn't been using the phone lately.

I don't have to wonder long, since without letting me go, Bianca starts to mumble into my hair.

"When you didn't answer, I was so worried about you."

I laugh, releasing all the tension that built up in my body while I was preparing for my arrest.

"I don't always answer the phone. It's not like there's a killer on the loose. He's still in custody, right? So you don't have to worry about me."

Her face blanches as she pulls away and stares into my eyes, grabbing my hands.

"They found another body, Zoey."

I quirk my head to the side, lifting one eyebrow. I'm truly puzzled.

"How? He's in jail, right?"

"Yes, but who knows how long that'll last? He's adamant he's innocent, and another murder... If it's the same M.O., well, maybe he isn't guilty after all. Maybe there's still a killer on the loose."

I don't speak. I can't. What she's saying is so wild but also makes complete sense.

"I heard over the radio that they found the body of a woman. No identifying markers, but she looked to be early thirties with blond hair. I tried not to worry, but I couldn't help it. I called you to ease my nerves, but when it went straight to voicemail, I freaked out. I came directly here to check on you," she says quickly, causing her to take in a sharp breath.

She finally releases my hands and embraces me again.

"I was so worried that it could have been you. I'm so happy that you're okay. Gosh, I'm so relieved. I can't imagine life without being able to see you anymore," she says, pulling away again with a tear in her eye.

"You're such a good friend! I'm okay. Relax now. I'm fine. Here, let's sit," I say, gesturing to the couch.

As we sink into the soft white cushions, I stare into space.

"Wow. Just wow," I comment, hoping that Bianca realizes I need some time to absorb what she's told me—but not for the reason she thinks, of course.

I've learned a lot from this encounter. Bianca is such a great friend, and she truly cares so deeply for me. More importantly, though, a murderer is on the loose. That means Bartholomew may not have seen me and won't rat me out. It also means the true killer may have seen me, though, since those notes are irrefutable proof that someone saw me somewhere I shouldn't have been.

Bianca's relieved that I'm safe, but I have no idea for how much longer that'll be true.

Chapter 22

A few days have passed, and I still find myself thinking back fondly on my best friend's reaction. I never expected her to be so worried about me. Her concern for me hasn't dwindled since the day they found that young woman's body. As a result, she checks on me more often, and I'm expected to respond ASAP so as not to worry her.

Her concerns make me feel ashamed. We were always friends, good friends, but there's no denying that I reached out again solely to learn more about the first murder. Yikes, I can't believe I have to think of them as Murder One and Murder Two.

I rekindled our friendship selfishly, and she cares about me so selflessly. I'm not a horrible friend, though. I'm not using her. I genuinely want to be her best friend again, and I'm committed to that. Especially now that I can see how deeply she cares for me.

As I'm driving, making my way toward my next delivery, a sudden thought crosses my mind. Maybe the second murder is a good thing for my case. I know for a fact that I am not responsible for the second murder and that I was not at the scene of the crime. Nothing links me to the second victim, and therefore it's unlikely the authorities would consider me guilty of one and not the other. Right? A girl can dream.

That's all I usually do as I drive—dream as I watch the houses pass by through my dirty, water-spotted, bug-streaked windows. I haven't had the time, energy, or mental fortitude to put any effort into keeping them clean lately.

Other than checking the delivery app and upcoming route occasionally, I zone out on autopilot, daydreaming and imagining. Since I've taken a break from house hunting, there's no need for me to focus and study the things around me. I told myself I'd try to pay more attention to my surroundings, but that was when I thought Lucas might be stalking me. With the new revelations and additional murder, well, now it seems very unlikely that he is.

I curse under my breath. I very likely still have a stalker, so I really should be more observant. The day's almost over, though, so I'll just have to start with fresh eyes tomorrow.

When I get back to the store, I pop my head in to tell Kristi goodbye.

"I'm done for the day!" I say with a wave, leaning my upper half in and only one foot through the door.

I want to be polite and tell her I'm going home, but I'm not in the mood for small talk.

"Oh, hey, before you go," she says, "I wanted to tell you about an unusual call I got earlier."

I pull my other leg over the threshold and let the door close slowly behind me. Guess I can't avoid it today, so I put on my newly perfected fake smile.

"Yeah?" I ask, trying to appear interested. Of course, the old me would be eager to hear about a sketchy phone call, and so I have to play the part. At least until I get all my baggage taken care of and can actually go back to being my old self.

"Yep. Don't want to freak you out or anything, but it was the cops."

I stare at her questioningly, hoping that I heard her wrong.

"Cops?" I ask, genuinely confused.

"Mhmm. I think he said his name was Detective Callais. He's investigating a case and said he saw you drive by. Wait, before you ask, no, I don't know which case or anything. He didn't say, and I didn't want to know.

"He spotted the company logo on your car and called to ask about my drivers. He specifically described your SUV, though, so I told him your name and how you're the main driver. I told him about how Maggie steps in when you're sick." With a nervous smile, she adds, "I also gave him your address." Then she says, "I mean, he's a cop! He asked, and I listened! I'm just following the law... I think." She appears to ponder her statement as her eyes dart to the left.

"No, no, yeah, that's okay," I manage to say, although my thoughts are bouncing around my head like gas molecules. "Did he say anything else? Like when he planned to come by?"

"I told him what time you usually get off, and he said he'd try to catch you at home after he made a few other stops," she says with a shrug.

"That's totally okay. I'm sure it's nothing."

I don't know if I'm saying it more to calm her or myself.

"Thanks, Kristi. Guess I'd better get home. Can't keep the cops waiting," I say in an attempt to sound cheery.

I enter my car slowly, lifting my leg into it. I'm in no rush to get home, and I need to practice being innocent. Practice appearing confused. How can I practice when I don't know what they want from me?

I breathe slowly, trying to reduce my anxiety so that I don't look suspiciously apprehensive to the police. Ugh, screw all this nonsense. I'll just play dumb and maintain my innocence. That's all I can do. I also need to try to avoid telling any lies so I can keep from getting caught in one, which can only make me look guilty.

I might show up shaking and nervous, but I'm sure the police are used to that. Even before all this started, I'd get nervous when I saw a cop car hiding on the bayou side, trying to catch unsuspecting speeders as they rounded a curve. I'd shake nervously, gripping the steering wheel, and watch them in my rearview mirror as I drove past, ensuring they wouldn't follow me, even though I wasn't actively doing anything wrong. I've always been intimidated by the police, for obvious reasons, but I can see how that's normal. It is normal, right?

Well, they know what time I get off work, and I'm sure they expected Kristi to let me know they wanted to talk to me, so I really shouldn't linger too long. That would look suspect. This is good, though—at least they aren't trying to arrest me. Surely they'd try harder to find me and not cater to my work schedule. The way Kristi explained it to me didn't sound too serious.

I drive home slowly, the cloudy sky hiding the sun away, but it's done nothing to decrease the temperature outside. I check to see that my brake tag sticker isn't expired, and at a red light, I even pull out my registration to make sure it's up to date. I don't know if detectives look at things like that, but I know I don't want to do anything wrong in their presence.

I manage to make the usual five-minute drive last for about seven minutes, and I'm relieved that no one is in my driveway when I arrive home. I pull in toward the left side of the driveway, as it gets me closer to my front door just in case those clouds transform into rain clouds before I get out.

I look behind me at the street, but I don't see any cop cars or unfamiliar vehicles parked in the street. I push out a breath and tell myself it's a good thing they're not eager and champing at the bit to talk to me. I'm not a top priority. Whatever this is about, it should be small potatoes.

Before the sky decides it wants to rain, I step out of the car, carrying my purse with me. As I go to close my car door, I hear an engine approaching. I pretend that I don't as I walk to my door and begin to unlock it.

Maybe it's just a neighbor coming home. Maybe the police don't need to talk to me anymore. Maybe, maybe, maybe.

Much to my dismay, I hear the sound of loose gravel crunch under tires, and without needing to look I can tell that there is a car pulling into my driveway. Before I push my door open, I turn around casually, hoping to appear the same as any innocent woman expecting the police to show up would act.

Should I smile? Would that be insincere? Narcissistic? Well, I'm playing clueless, so a smile is acceptable, I think to myself as I plaster one on my face as the unmarked police car doors open. Two police officers, well technically maybe detectives, as they aren't in police uniforms, step out from each side of the vehicle.

"Ms. Zoey Bergeron?" the driver of the car says to me without coming closer to me.

"Yes?" I can't help the inflection in my tone, so my answer sounds more like a question.

"I'm Detective Callais," he says, touching his chest before gesturing to the woman on the other side of the car. "This is Detective Gisclair. We'd like to ask you for a moment of your time."

"That's fine. I'm just getting home. Please, come in," I say as I beckon them toward me. I turn away from them and use the moment I open the door to look up in silent prayer.

Let's get this over with.

Chapter 23

I gesture toward the couch as the officers enter the house behind me. I wish I'd had time to light a candle, but at least I replaced the floral plug-in next to the door when I cleaned up last time so that an aroma of clean linen floats in the air.

"Please have a seat. Can I get y'all anything to drink?" I ask, pretending to be the picture of a nonchalant hostess.

Detective Gisclair shakes her head just as Detective Callais says, "No, but thank you."

I sit in the reclining chair that I hardly ever use as they take their seats on my couch, opposite from me.

I don't want to make the first statement for fear that they'll take it the wrong way and skew my words, but I don't want to be weird and quiet either.

"May I ask what this is about?" I say, tilting my head.

I feel like that's surely an appropriate question that anyone in my position would ask. I slacken my shoulders and try not to seem nervous as the detectives look at one another and then turn back to me.

I hope they don't think I'm trying too hard to seem relaxed.

Detective Callais clears his throat before speaking.

"I'm sure you've heard about the recent murders we've had in town. As you can imagine, we are thoroughly investigating each in an attempt to determine the identity of the killer and bring justice to the families of the victims, as well as to prevent any more murders in our area."

I nod my head to indicate that I understand, but again, I don't offer up anything that might incriminate me.

Just then, my phone vibrates in my pocket, but I ignore the sensation.

Instead of jumping into his next spiel, Detective Callais pauses, which I believe is his way of giving me another opportunity to say something.

He didn't ask a question, so as far as I'm concerned, he doesn't need an answer.

"Now, please understand that you haven't done anything wrong and we are just doing our jobs to obtain as much information as possible. We believe you may have been in or around the area of one or more of the crime scenes," he says, breaking eye contact with me.

I avoid backing down and looking away. I can't do anything too suspicious.

My jaw drops, and I lift my hand gently to cover my mouth, which I then close. I drop my hand down to my lap, maintaining eye contact with Detective Callais.

"Am I in danger?"

"We can't be sure. We are aware your job requires you to be on the road, and after speaking to your employer, we have reason to believe you may have seen something that may be relevant to our investigation."

Whew, I mentally sigh with relief. Not audibly, of course. So they don't suspect me. They're here to ask me for my help. This is great!

I paint a confused and thoughtful look on my face, or at least

I try.

"Hmm, let me think," I say as I tap my chin.

I almost tell them that no, I haven't, but I'm glad I don't, because I've just realized that although I know where the first murder occurred, I know very little about the second one.

"Could you kindly remind me in what general area both murders took place?"

He smiles at me, and I feel like I've passed a test. This bastard. I know he's only doing his job, but he's hoping that I'll slip up. I wonder if he treats everyone he interviews as if they could be a suspect.

Detective Gisclair opens a notepad and reads two different addresses to me.

"Oh yes, I remember seeing the crime scene tape at one of those houses," I say as I look up and try to place the second address in relation to my route. Then the realization dawns on me. "Wow. The second address isn't directly on my route, but it is in one of the neighborhoods I deliver to."

"Precisely. Take your time, but please think back to both locations and the surroundings over these past couple of weeks, or even days. Have you noticed anything of note? A strange car, or an unfamiliar face, perhaps?" Detective Callais prods.

"Hmm, let me think..." I say, trailing off. I do think then. Have I seen anything?

After what I deem a reasonable amount of time, I lift my chin and look at the detectives.

"I have no idea if this is the information you're looking for, but now that I think of it, I did see something before the first murder took place. I can't be sure of the exact day or time, but I saw a lawn care guy pulling away from the curb. I only really noticed because the yards didn't look all that great, and

I thought to myself that it was unusual for him to be there and not cutting their grass."

"Anything else?" Callais asks me, like what I just told him wasn't important or worthy of note, although I know darn well it was.

"Yikes, I really can't think of anything at the moment. I'm sorry."

"No need for apologies," Gisclair chimes in.

"I'm curious about something, though," Callais says, his eyes boring into me. "Did you ever call and report that information when the murder became public knowledge?"

My mouth is so dry I struggle to swallow.

"I've really only just thought about it now that you're asking me," I say, tilting my head. "At the time, it struck me as a little peculiar, but in no way did I think of it as an alarming detail."

"What about after you saw the crime scene tape?" Callais asks. "Why didn't you call and report it then?"

I look at him with feigned confusion.

"I didn't believe for a second that an unfamiliar lawn care specialist scoping out potential clients was guilty of murder. My mind just doesn't work like that," I say defensively, trying not to sound too insincere.

His intimidating stare continues for seconds before he replaces it with a smile of understanding.

"Of course. Can you describe the man that you saw?"

"Oh my, that was so long ago. He was a man—of that much I'm sure. I'm sorry. I don't even know if it's relevant. Even at the time, I didn't pay attention. It struck me as different but not unusual, you know?"

Hearing myself say this out loud makes me realize that the information I have could be pretty incriminating. I just don't know where to stop telling them my truth. I don't want to say too much accidentally.

It's very likely Bartholomew did kill that man after all; I just don't understand how he committed the second murder if he was in custody.

"His hair wasn't long, and with the cap, I'm not even sure what color it was. No facial hair, either, I think," I throw in for good measure.

"I see. No other identifying markers? Birthmarks, tattoos, eyeglasses? What about his height?"

"I'm sorry, Detective Callais. As I said, it really seemed so inconsequential at the time. I really didn't notice much else," I say, pursing my lips into a flat line in an attempt to appear apologetic.

"Nothing else about either area sticks out to you? Anything at all?" Callais pries.

"No, sorry," I say with a grimace.

He slaps his palms on his thighs as he sits up, Gisclair following suit.

"Please, if you have anything that comes to mind, especially about something in relation to the second murder victim, I kindly ask that you let me know," Callais says as he hands me a business card.

"I absolutely will. Truly, I'll spend the evening rummaging through my head, trying to think of any detail or difference. No matter how insignificant it seems."

He shakes my hand as I stand up to join him and his partner.

"You can text me anytime. Don't feel like anything you have to say doesn't hold merit. No difference is too small when we are trying to stop a murderer."

I shake Detective Gisclair's hand as she walks by me, and I

follow both officers to the door.

"Thank you for your help, Ms. Bergeron."

I offer them a sympathetic smile as they walk down the driveway and back to their car. I continue to linger in the doorway and wave goodbye as they leave.

As they disappear, I breathe a sigh of relief, grateful the unexpected interrogation is finally over.

Chapter 24

After the detectives leave, I sit with my tormenting thoughts. How can this be my real life? I did nothing to deserve all these mixed emotions, horrendous thoughts, and underhanded accusations.

No, the officers didn't technically accuse me of anything, but there was definitely an undertone of malice throughout that whole conversation. I told them what they wanted to hear, and I felt like it still wasn't good enough. I can't blame them. They were simply doing their jobs. I want them to do that.

What if, in some crazy way, Bartholomew isn't the killer? That could very likely be true, based on the second murder. The police have to find the real killer.

I'm lucky to be alive. I was in both areas where people were murdered. Either victim could just as easily have been me. I need the authorities to find the killer so that the locals and I can all go on and live our lives without fear of being murdered.

I think back to the second address the detectives mentioned to me. Of course, I've been trying to be more cognizant of my surroundings, so surely I've noticed something. Nothing is coming to my mind. With my thoughts swirling, I can't focus.

Usually, when I forget what I've been doing or can't remember something, I retrace my steps. Yes, I can do that now! I can drive my route, take the same way near the area of the second murder, and see if the location jogs my memory!

I check the time on my phone, and I notice the missed-call notification from earlier.

Bianca called me, but she didn't leave a voicemail. As I close out the call log, I notice that I also have a text. I open it to see that it, too, is from Bianca.

BeeOnka: *HEADS UP. Don't freak out, but some guys from the station want to ask you some questions.*

Thanks, Bianca. A little late, though.
   I text her back.

Zoey: *All good. I have nothing to hide. YOU KNOW ME!*

Although she's only a desk sergeant, her warning tells me she has access to details about the case. I take that thought and put it in my back pocket for later just in case I need it.

It's not too late, almost five o'clock, so I think I will go and retrace my steps after all. I'm nosy as hell, too, but I won't go directly to the crime scene. If anyone saw me, they'd go telling the police and involve me yet again. I'll stick to my route, and even if someone does notice and rats me out, I can admit I was doing my civic duty, trying to jog my memory in hopes of helping the police find the killer.

I quickly run out to my car and jump in, trying to avoid the mosquitoes that are already starting to invade as the bright sun begins to fade from the sky. It's not dark enough for me to need my headlights yet, though, which is good for what I need to do. I want to retrace my steps in as familiar a fashion as possible, and doing it in the dark simply won't suffice.

Rather than start at the coffee shop, I head in the general direction I need to go. I don't want it to be too dark before I get there. My skin feels clammy, so I reach forward and turn on the air conditioning, the hum of the system coming to life cutting through the silence. The radio's turned off, and I keep it that way because I need to focus.

At first, nothing sticks out to me, and nothing that I see triggers any memories of unfamiliar faces. At one point, I get close to the crime scene, perhaps just a street away, but even then, nothing. The farther away I get, the more I realize that coming here was a mistake. I haven't remembered anything, because there is nothing to remember.

I pull up at a stop sign, looking to my left and then my right and then quickly back to my left again. Not because I see a car coming but because this is the spot where I usually see that woman walking with her dog. I haven't seen her this week, and I almost always catch her around this stop sign.

I blew off her absence earlier. What if there was a deeper reason that she wasn't there, though? What if she was the second murder victim? What if the young man I saw her talking to what seemed like forever ago was the one who killed her?

At the time, I made up a silly little fake scenario, just like usual. But what if it came true? I take a left and pull over to the side of the road, outside a somewhat ramshackle two-story house. It must have lost a battle during one of the more recent hurricanes, the owners probably unable to come up with the money to renovate.

I don't think I have to worry about someone getting upset with me for parking in their yard as I examine the boarded-up windows and the tattered blue tarp that covers the roof, rising at the corners as it catches the light breeze.

If that woman, the one I'd often see walking on my route, was the one that was murdered, why? Why do both of these cases hit so close to home for me? That can't be a coincidence, right? Is the killer intentionally choosing people on my coffee route? Is the killer following me and wanting me to know that they are? Is it just that we live in a small town and it's truly a coincidence? Am I actually crazy? I hate that the thought crosses my mind, but it does. I recently discovered on a podcast that I'm essentially around the age schizophrenia can develop. Add that to my list of ongoing concerns.

I search the internet on my phone, desperate to see who the last victim was. Why didn't I look sooner? I click on a link to a recent news article, and I almost drop my phone as the image of the victim appears on my screen. I see the scar and understand instantly that the woman in the photo is the exact one on my mind. Her name's Abby Roberts. I was so absorbed in my own drama that I never even realized her information was released to the public.

Now I'm left with more questions. This time around, I have some that I can answer, but I'm not sure how. Do I text the detective and let him know that I've seen her along my route? I don't see why not. I think doing so can only help my case. He gave me an attitude for not coming forth sooner about details he considered crucial to the investigation.

Should I also mention the young man I saw before? He could very well be some innocent guy and not a crazy killer. I don't even remember enough about him to describe him to the detectives. They'd likely never find him unless they knew things I didn't know. Which is very probable.

I think I'll sleep on it. I'll tell the detective tomorrow. I feel as if reaching out now, hardly an hour after the officers' departure from my house, may make it seem like I've been hiding information. I don't want it to appear as if I'm trying to divert attention away from myself, when in reality I've merely jogged my memory with a road trip.

I think I know exactly what I need to do, so I text Lucas to meet me at my house.

When I get home, he's already there, and the sun has officially left the sky alone. Now darkness hangs overhead, with the only light on the ground cast by the moon.

"Hey, gorgeous," he says to me as I step out of the car.

"Hello, handsome," I coo back while a blush spreads across my cheeks.

I watch him then, savoring every detail. His square glasses reflect the glare of distant streetlights as he sits atop his motorcycle.

That was why I texted him. There's something so freeing about riding a motorbike with nothing but the wind barraging my ears, the force of it whipping my hair around erratically, and my favorite part—my arms wrapped around his waist as I hold on to him tightly.

Some one-on-one time with him, the scent of his cologne surrounding me, and the freedom of the open road may dull my racing thoughts and grant me the serenity to dream of his embrace long after he's gone.

Chapter 25

The next morning, I awake with some of the heaviness lifted from my chest. I can almost still smell Lucas's cologne, even though he didn't follow me inside after dropping me off. I could tell he wanted to, but he didn't push when I didn't invite him in. I really am trying to slow things down this time around, although it isn't easy. I dreamt of him last night, but that was nothing new. I've dreamt about him since the day I met him. I lived for the moments he'd visit me in my dreams, but now, I can actualize my dreams with him back in my life.

Before we started speaking again, it was blissful to see him in my sleep, since I didn't allow myself the luxury of being with him in the waking world. The dreams were also a torment—to go from feeling like he was there with me to realizing that he wasn't, followed by the finality of knowing that we'd never be together again.

Why must dreams feel so real? The urge to contact him on those mornings... the mornings he visited me in my dreams... was always the start of a hard day. The tease that I could be with him, only to have it ripped away by reality, never made for a peaceful day.

I'd think of so many excuses to reach out on those days, unable to get him off my mind. I'd even start typing up the text, like, "Hey, what was the name of that band you told me about?" or "Did you sign up for softball again this year?" However, I never allowed myself to reach out to him. I was steadfast in my decision. Now, as I lie down in my bed, staring up at the ceiling fan's never-ending rotation, I smile, knowing that I don't have to resist the urge anymore. I can text him just like we used to, and so I grab my phone and I go to do just that.

As I turn on my phone, I see a notification indicating an unread text. Lucas texted me before I even woke up.

Loo-Kiss: *Good morning, darling! I was hoping to dream of you after last night, but I had no luck. Guess I'll have to see you in person soon instead.*

In an instant, I realize we'll be the grossly affectionate couple people love to mock.

Still, I needed these emotions. I needed a little light to bring me out of the depths of despair. I hope this lightheartedness continues. I hope the police find the killer soon so this can all finally be over.

I need to text Callais today, though, and I may as well do it now and get it over with. I begrudgingly throw the covers off me and move to slide out of bed and into my bedside slippers. One of them is there, but the other seems to have slipped under the bed. I jump off the bed and look underneath to find the slipper flipped upside down underneath, which is slightly peculiar, since I remember taking them both off and lining them up in preparation for the morning, as I always do.

I got up to pee last night, so I'm sure that in my haste, I just accidentally kicked the slipper. Other, more insidious reasons for its movement begin to come to the forefront of my mind.

Man, I could really use that camera. I make a mental note to check the tracking later to find out when I can expect it to be delivered.

With my bare foot, I pull the slipper out and then put it on before scurrying to the kitchen to find the card Mr. Callais left. Is it rude to call him Mister? Are detectives like doctors in that way, expecting you to refer to them by their distinguished titles? I may just err on the side of caution and call him Detective to his face—if I have to see his face again, that is.

I try not to overthink it. I just want to let him know I thought of something, and I'll let him make his own conclusions.

Zoey: *Hi, this is Zoey Bergeron. I've thought of something else. Please give me a call when you have a moment.*

There, that's done. I head to the kitchen to pour a cup of water so that I can prepare my voice for a phone conversation just in case he calls soon. Good thing I do because just as I take a sip, my phone starts to ring, with the detective's number visible on the caller ID.

I clear my throat before I answer.

"Hello?" I reply, as if I didn't just text him asking to call me.

"Yes, Zoey? How are you today?"

Oh, so he does have manners.

"Fine, and you?"

"As good as can be expected. Listen, could you come down to the station?"

I freeze.

"Oh, sir, it's nothing crazy. I just thought of a little something. You know, like you said, any small detail might count."

"Yes, which is why I'd like you to come in. We'd like to hear more from you."

"Oh, well, I don't know how much more helpful I'll be."

"Please, Ms. Bergeron. We won't take much of your time."

I know I shouldn't, but I say it anyway.

"Should I contact a lawyer?"

He laughs at my question, but his reaction doesn't sound genuine. No, this laugh sounds more like he's trying to disarm me.

"That isn't necessary! Truly, just stop by whenever you have a moment today."

"Yes, sir, of course I will. See you later."

I groan as I hang up the phone. I just had to go and say something. Great. Lord knows what they're thinking over there. They probably have very little in the way of leads and are looking over everything with a fine-toothed comb.

I don't know what they're thinking, but I know someone who does.

I'll go get dressed and stop at Bianca's on my way. Today is Saturday, so I'm pretty sure she's off from work.

After I slip on a light summer dress, which I think will pair well with the excruciating heat of south Louisiana, I head for the door, scooping up my phone and purse as I do. I reach out to turn the doorknob, and it rotates easily, without me having to switch off the lock.

Did I leave the door unlocked last night? I pull the knob toward me, and, sure enough, the door opens with ease. I can't believe I did something so foolish with a killer on the loose. I slap my forehead. I really need to stop doing stupid stuff like that. It's a miracle I'm not dead yet. I push my mistake from my mind. It's not the first time I've done that, but I really need to shape up. Now is not the time.

Things moving around with no explanation. Mysterious notes. I'm practically begging for trouble, making such a stupid mistake.

As I walk out the door, I see Eric near his mailbox. We make eye contact immediately, almost as if he's been watching my door. He starts to quickly, and quite nervously, lift his hands to check his mailbox as he averts his eyes.

Why must he make every encounter awkward? I nod to him as he walks back up the path to his door, his shoulders slumped as he scurries toward his home. He doesn't look back at me, though, which is fine by me.

Just ten minutes after I leave my house and make sure I lock my door, I pull into Bianca's neighborhood. She lives in one of the nicest and newest subdivisions around town.

I would never dream of entering these homes for my extracurricular activities. There are way too many cameras here, and rightly so, since these people have expensive possessions they wish to keep.

As I navigate my way through the neighborhood, I admire the elegant motor homes and boats that rest on trailers in many driveways. I observe well-kept lawns as far as the eye can see, as well as some expensive-looking go-carts and four-wheelers.

Bianca's house is no different. Her home is one of the smaller ones, since she and her fiancé, Chuck, have no children. Her white-paneled house, which has a black roof, is also one of the more modern homes in the subdivision. She always jokes that she can keep up with trends because she doesn't have to keep up with kids.

Luckily, her car's in the driveway. Chuck's truck is here, too, but he works offshore, so that doesn't necessarily mean that he's home and I'm about to disturb the couple's Saturday morning, which I hope I'm not.

I barely finish knocking on the door before it swings open.

"Well, well, well," Bianca tells me as she gestures for me to enter. "What a surprise!"

"Sorry to bother you. But you won't believe where I'm about to go."

We stand there in her foyer, and I can tell she's eager to see why I've stopped by unannounced. Maybe that's a good thing?

"Where?" she asks as she rests her palm on her mahogany entry table.

"The police station! On your day off, of all days," I say, keeping my eyes on her so that I can analyze her reaction.

She looks shocked. Great. Maybe this is just a little visit for information and not the beginning of my journey to false imprisonment.

"I thought the detectives stopped by yesterday? Isn't Callais sort of dreamy?"

I raise an eyebrow at her. No, I do not think the detective asking questions about a murder scene at which I was present but wasn't supposed to be is "dreamy." But I can't tell her that.

"I've never been questioned by the police before! The last thing I thought about was how attractive he was."

She giggles.

"I'm just messing with you! You seem kind of flustered."

I roll my eyes.

"Well, that's because I kind of am. You know I'm as innocent as they come, but I have a weird complex when it comes to cops. I'm always scared they'll fuss at me, even though I'm not doing anything wrong."

"Well, we can delve into your apparent childhood trauma at a later date. You're fine. They just know that you work in the area, and they don't know much else about anything. Trust me. I take the call line for tips, and we hardly have anybody calling in with anything!"

I release an audible sigh.

"Okay, okay. I knew you'd make me feel better. So, I'm not, like, circled in red at the top of some triangle they have on a giant bulletin board?"

Now it's her turn to roll her eyes at me.

"No, girl. Now go and get that over with so we can maybe do margaritas later," she says with a wink, shooing me out the door.

I turn and look at her smiling face through the glass door as I get back into my car.

Chapter 26

The police station is just as intimidating as I imagined it. It doesn't help that it's nestled within the courthouse. A vile green paint adorns the walls, and the furniture seems outdated. The few small windows let hardly any light in, and the cones of sunlight that do shine through illuminate the particles of dust that litter the air.

Bianca's absence from the desk fills me with dread. I'd feel a lot better if she were the one sitting there behind the desk and at the gates of hell to welcome me. Her counterpart sits there instead, barely looking up from her crossword puzzle as I approach.

She must sense me there, though, because before I can even clear my throat to get her attention, she speaks.

"How may I help you today?"

"Umm, Detective Callais asked me to come in."

"I'll let him know. Please have a seat," she says without even asking my name or making me sign in.

This introduction seems very nonchalant, so either they don't have any quarrel with me or they're just trying to throw me off my guard.

I wait only two minutes before I hear heavy footsteps approach from the hallway located to the left of the waiting room.

I look up from my twisting hands and make eye contact with Detective Callais.

"Thanks for coming in, Zoey. As I said, we'll try not to take up too much of your time," he says as he gestures for me to follow. We don't have to walk very far past the open doors lining the gloomily painted hallway until we arrive at a closed one on the right.

I take in a sharp breath when I see what lies beyond the door. I was expecting his office, with him sitting behind his desk and Detective Gisclair waiting for me to join. Instead, I see an interrogation room.

The walls are dark gray, and one lone table stands in the middle of the room; single chairs sit across from one another. I'm disappointed to discover the absence of a two-way mirror. Guess that must only be in the movies.

Detective Callais motions for me to sit in the chair nearest the door as he closes it behind us. The door slams shut, and the sound makes me jump off the chair as soon as I sit.

Luckily, he doesn't seem to have noticed as he flips through a notepad before setting it down gently on the table.

A military-style haircut frames his head, and he furrows his brows in concentration as he reads some of the notes on the page. I avert my eyes from the notepad, although I'm dying to know what kinds of things he has written there.

"Zoey," he says, looking up from the notepad and locking eyes with me, "I feel like there's more that you aren't telling me."

Oh no, no, no. This can't be happening. He said I didn't need a lawyer! The bastard lied to me!

Instead of showing my fear, I plaster a look of confusion on my face.

"I'm sorry?"

"We know you must have seen something. Some details that we can use. I'll be real with you here. We think we know who the killer is, but we could be wrong, and we don't want to convict an innocent man. We've spoken with your boss, and, after canvassing the area, we think you are the most likely person to have seen something. Please, try your best to recall anything, anything at all," he pleads.

I draw my lips together to the right and avert my eyes, pretending to search my brain for information. I know what he wants, and it would help him. It could help prove Bartholomew's guilt and prevent me from being considered a suspect. After all, Callais has just said he doesn't want to convict an innocent person falsely.

"Well, now that I think about it, I believe his truck—well, it was dark green."

I stumble over my words, putting on a performance as if I'm just dredging up these details from a hazy past.

"He had a white closed-in trailer with the image of a riding lawnmower on the side. I'm sorry. I didn't notice the name. The man, well, he had on some khaki pants and maybe a blue shirt? Ball cap on his head, too, if I remember correctly."

I look at him to determine if I've given him enough details. It feels good to tell the truth and not have to worry about being caught in a lie.

Should I go further? Should I tell him about the notes? Now I don't have to feign my attempts to think, because my gears are spinning with all the things I could say. The detectives would believe anything I said, but it wouldn't be fair to make things up. I don't want to skew or interfere with the investigation. I just want to ensure my safety. I don't want the police to know that I was there, and if they have a suspect and evidence... well, they won't keep looking now, will they?

They won't find anything involving me in either murder, so I'll be free to transition back to how my life was before all this got stirred up. Even better than before, because I'll have Lucas.

I act shocked, my jaw dropping as if I've just had an epiphany.

"I was far away, but I think that as I was heading toward him, he was walking away from the house? I glanced at the house as I passed, and I saw what I think was a note on the door. Yes, a note on the door. What if it was a threat? What if I could have prevented it..." My voice fades, and I try to force tears to my eyes, but I can't.

"Oh my god," I say. "Is that man dead because of me?"

Now I don't have to fake tears. They fall from my face. I cry for the dead man who I felt like I knew but never really did. I cry for his family having lost him and the horrible way in which he was killed.

"Zoey, you know there was no way you could have known."

I look at Callais through the tears that now cloud my vision. He looks as placid as he always does.

I use my fingers to wipe my tears away, since I saw no tissues on the empty table when the detective and I entered the room.

"Besides, not until this moment did you even remember that," he says, "so obviously, nothing you could have done would have changed anything."

"I guess you're right. It's just all so horrible. All of it."

"As you can imagine, we need eyewitness details for the second murder as well. Can you remember anything pertinent?"

"Yes, the reason I texted you was because I saw a young man near the house of the second murder," I say before going on to provide a description.

I tell him everything confidently, once again relishing in the fact that I don't have to lie.

Chapter 27

After a few more inquiries, Detective Callais thanks me and lets me walk out of the police station. By then, I'm feeling a little lighter.

I race home to meet Lucas, since my camera has finally come in and he is going to help me set it up.

When I get home, he's already standing right outside, holding a package that I presume contains a camera.

"Package acquired," he says, smiling at me as I lean in to kiss his cheek.

"Thank you! I tried to get an easy one to set up, but you know I'll find any excuse to get you in my vicinity!"

"Oh, that reminds me. You look resplendent today."

"Thank you! Now put that box down and give me one of those hugs I've been missing!"

As his arms envelop me, so does his scent. Just like that, the tension falls from my body, and I'm practically floating.

"I appreciate your help. You've always been good with technology, so I figured this was right up your alley," I say as I pry myself from his arms.

"Oh yeah. Not only do I enjoy it, but I also enjoy seeing you."

How did I ever think this man was a stalker? He may be obsessed with me, but I'm just as obsessed with him.

"Oh, stop, you're making me blush! Let's get it set up. Now I know it sounds crazy, but I don't want to set it up outside," I say as I walk toward my front door to let us in.

As we enter, the flow of conditioned air cools my skin instantly, a stark contrast to the heat outside.

"Why inside?" He looks at me, perplexed.

"Maybe I'm crazy, but I've been noticing random things misplaced around the house. If someone else lived here, I could easily blow it off. It's just me, though, so it's been kind of disturbing. I really just wanted the camera for peace of mind."

"Hmm. Have you had friends over? Other guys?" he asks with a wink.

"No! No guys. I did have some friends over, but I don't know—I still want to put it up. Gosh, I hope to the heavens I don't actually catch some guy skulking around on it! I want to see nothing and ease my mind so I can sleep a little better at night."

"I could help you sleep," he says, nudging me.

"Ever the flirt, Lucas!" I say, waving him off. Playfully, I continue, "Get to work! Given what I need it for... where do you think I should put it?"

"Well, I want to say directly at the door, but then there's a lot of the house that gets left out of the image. Maybe in the living room. That way, you'll get footage of a broader area of the house. That's what you want to see, right? If someone is moving stuff around?" he asks me for clarification.

I nod.

"This way," he says, "no matter what they do, you should at least get them making their way to whatever they end up messing with. Does that sound reasonable to you?"

"Yes, absolutely."

"I've got to say that I'm concerned that you don't feel safe inside your own home, though," he says as he starts opening the package containing the camera.

"I'm probably being paranoid. One way to help is to get this camera set up. I'm fine, truly. Don't worry about me."

He stares at me, like he's trying to determine if I'm lying, before giving me a sidelong glance and turning his back to me so that he can begin setting up my new home security device.

To break the silence, I tell him, "I just have been feeling 'off' lately. I just want things to go back to normal."

I feel safe with him, so I decide to be a little vulnerable.

"Those murders... I can't get them out of my head. To think something so serious is happening and may continue until they catch the guy. He could be next door. He could be any guy you pass on the street, and we don't know."

"What makes you think it's a guy?" he asks, almost sounding offended.

"Come on. You know what I mean. 'Guy' comes out naturally, but of course it could be a woman, although I think that would be pretty far-fetched, don't you? We get our first serial killer in forever, and also it's a woman? Hard to believe but possible. It is always possible."

"I'm just giving you a hard time. But this right here"—he taps at the shelf on which he has nestled the camera into my entertainment center—"this wasn't hard at all. Let me see your phone. I'll download the app so you can review the footage."

He guides me through it all, and I learn to navigate the app easily. It's perfect. It doesn't have all the bells and whistles, and it doesn't need to. I need it for reassurance.

Sadly, Lucas doesn't stay long, but I get it. I popped into his life out of nowhere. I can't expect him to dedicate every second of his life to me. Actually, I hope we don't fall back into that nasty habit.

I remember then to text Kaci, Sierra, and Bianca to see if we're going to meet up for margaritas before the day ends. I must split my time among them evenly on this occasion.

With the camera installed, the video footage easily accessible on my phone, and my brief encounter with Lucas, I feel a strong sense of calmness seize me. I might actually be able to sleep tonight.

Chapter 28

Having the camera has been great. Since Lucas set it up, nothing has changed, and I wonder if the camera's presence is why. So far, the footage I've reviewed has been unremarkable. Whether the installation of the camera is a placebo effect for my mind or actually a deterrent... well, I don't like to think about it.

The following Monday, a text from Bianca comes through just as I'm making my way home from work. I check the message eagerly, wondering if she wants to hang out soon, and I'm rewarded when I see that's exactly what she wants to do.

I tell her to come over after her shift as I enter the house.

I'd clean up before Bianca's arrival, but there really isn't much to clean, so I just put on some music to cut the silence and wait for her to appear. I have to wait only an hour or so before I hear her knock at the door.

I begin to step toward it, but she opens it and walks in before I can even get to it. Then she closes the door, leans her back against it, and faces me.

"I know I said I shouldn't talk about the case, but wow, guess what I learned today?"

We both stand there facing one another, she in her official drab work attire and me in my jeans and polo, as I wait patiently for her to answer. The faint scent of lavender wafts from her and enters my nostrils as I stare at her, indicating my confusion with a crooked half smile.

"I don't know. What?"

"They found DNA evidence at the first crime scene, which is crazy," she explains, her eyes growing as she continues. "They didn't have anything to hold Bartholomew, so they did a last-ditch do-over at the crime scene, and they found blond hair!" She opens her arms, and her fingers flail. "Like, what? So they tried to match it to known family members of the victim, his friends, and Barty boy, and *nothing*! No match. They basically have to let him go because they don't have enough evidence to hold him."

I'm silent as I listen to everything she says, thinking about the repercussions of knowing the details she tells me.

"So it's not Bartholomew, but they don't know who it is?"

"Back to square one," she replies with a shrug.

"I need to sit down," I say as I walk toward the couch, Bianca trailing me.

"This is chaos. We aren't equipped for this kind of thing. Stuff like this doesn't happen here," she says, more to herself than to me.

"What do you mean?"

"We aren't New Orleans, or Chicago, for that matter. We don't see these cases, ever. Those detectives are trying, but they're way out of their depth. At this point, we almost have to hope the killer goes maniac and does something stupid enough to land him in custody. Or hope that they stop killing, or go somewhere else," she huffs.

"So the DNA doesn't match anything they have in their system?" I ask for clarification.

"Nope. The cops have little pieces of the big picture, but that's it. They're missing too many puzzle pieces."

"Wow," I say, unable to add anything else, just staring into the air.

"Agreed. Just wow."

"How do you know?"

"The station was buzzing. Everyone's talking about it. I wanted you to know and be aware. I want you to be safe. To be careful. Okay?"

"Yes, thanks," I say, offering a bashful smile. "You be safe too."

"I won't keep you. I just stopped on the way home," she says, embracing me. "Everything will be fine. It'll all be over eventually," she mumbles into my ear before she pulls away.

I escort her to the door, and I'm really hoping that she's right, that this situation will end sooner rather than later.

If she'd stay longer, she could act as a dam to the inevitable raucous thoughts that are beginning to form in my mind, but I won't keep her. Chuck's probably home.

I close the door and head straight to my room. I throw myself onto the bed and lie there, looking up at the ceiling, my arms and legs spread wide.

They found a hair. The hair doesn't match Bartholomew's. They'll let him go. Police will search for another suspect. A killer's on the loose.

The worst thought, the one that keeps popping up, knocking and knocking, waiting to be acknowledged...

What if that hair is mine?

My DNA isn't in any system that I know of, so if the hair is mine, it makes sense for the police not to have a match. The police were able to find me easily, so what if they find someone who saw me, just like I saw Bartholomew? I'll be required to submit my DNA. If it ends up matching, well, that's all they need to lock me up forever, no matter how innocent I am or the ferocity with which I'll plead my case.

I will very likely be falsely convicted of murder.

God...

What if they accuse me of the second murder as well? I don't think I have an alibi; I'm almost always home alone. Bianca said it herself. It's chaos, they don't know what they're doing, and I'm the perfect target. They could blame that homicide on me, even though they only have a little evidence to support it. With Bartholomew officially off the hook, I can't even blame it on him like I thought I could.

Even if the police don't think it's me, I know they will throw me to the wolves. The cops need a scapegoat.

I repeat my mantra now more than ever, trying to push the fear from my mind.

You did nothing wrong.

At this point, I can only hope that the hair the police have found isn't mine and that they don't discover any more breadcrumbs that lead them to my door again.

Chapter 29

I've been feeling a little crazy, so why not act a little crazy?

I need to talk to Bartholomew. I shoot up from the bed as the thought comes to me, blond hair flying everywhere. I don't even think. Immediately, I grab my phone and try to search for something, anything that could tell me where I might be able to find him.

I could go to where he works. Today is a weekday, after all, but will he even be there after being imprisoned for so long? I'm sure he has a list of things he needs to catch up on and sort out, but that won't deter me. His place of work is my best option.

Without thinking, I slide on my slippers and head for the door, which I barely remember to lock behind me. The heat of the day falls on me like a curtain, and it's even hotter inside my car, as the stale air has sat baking in my absence.

I turn on the engine and immediately throw it into reverse. I'm familiar with the busy street in town that's home to Ledet's Landscaping, so I make my way.

The day isn't over yet, but just as my job doesn't follow a typical schedule, his may not either. I know you can't cut grass at night, so I think there's a chance I can catch him if he's there.

A few trucks litter the parking lot of the small building. His business is similar to Coffee Beams in that way—not a lot of foot traffic, but the operation still needs a home base for invoicing and parts, probably.

The air inside the car had just begun to cool off, but I allow the heat to rush back in as I step out and make my way toward the glass double doors of the small steel building. That glass is reflective, so I can't see inside, but I can see the determined look on my face, the wild baby hairs sticking out erratically from my head, and the fuzzy pink bedroom slippers on my feet.

Whoever is here, I'm about to give them something to talk about. I probably should have thought this idea through, though, since I'm not exactly flying under the radar like I should.

"Too late now," I whisper to myself as I pull on the door handle, hoping that I can get inside.

Luckily, as I pull, the door opens, and I can see that the interior is relatively empty, but that won't last long—a bell chimes above my head, alerting anyone here to my presence.

I don't have to wait long before I hear hesitant footsteps from around the corner to my left.

Bartholomew peeks his head nervously around that corner, and he looks confused.

"May I help you?"

He doesn't seem to recognize me or know who I am. I don't think he does, at least.

Jeez, what am I supposed to even say?

Hey, could you plead guilty to the murder you committed so that I don't have to suffer the consequences of your mistake?

Yeah. That won't work.

"Umm, hi? Could I have a moment of your time?" I ask, with a slight quiver in my voice.

"Sure? What about exactly?" he asks me, raising one eyebrow in question.

He's a big guy; his huge arms are crossed over his chest and rest on his potbelly, and a black baseball cap casts shadows over the top half of his face.

"I'm just going to come right out and say it. I want to know more about Alan Hebert's murder."

"You a reporter?"

I look down at my attire before looking back up to meet his eyes.

"Do I look like a reporter?"

"Not one I've ever seen," he says with a chuckle.

"I'm just a concerned citizen. Call me an amateur sleuth, if you will." The lies just start to spill from my mouth. "I've been following the case closely, and I can't imagine why they even considered you as a suspect in the first place. Can you tell me why?"

"Lady, I've been through a lot, okay? Are you serious right now?"

"Please. Just a few questions and I won't bother you again."

He stares at me, pondering what I've just said, before releasing his arms and leaning on the front counter next to him.

"Okay, I guess. Well, it's stupid, really. Guy owed me for a cut I did a while back. It's mostly me here, so I was late sorting through invoices and bills. As soon as I noticed, I went to his house to let him know, but he wasn't home. I left a note, and the cops found it. Called it 'incriminating evidence,'" he says, making air quotes for that last part.

"That's all they had on you?"

"Essentially, yes, but they kept me forever. The whole time they were trying to get more on me, but I didn't do nothing, so there was nothing to find."

"Did you know anything, like who might have actually done it?"

"Nothing. I was oblivious. You'd think being innocent of the crime would show through, but they didn't care. They wanted me to take the fall for it. Treated me like I did it, no matter how many times I told them I didn't."

"That's not fair."

"No, it isn't. I didn't kill that guy, but just because I got caught doing some sketchy stuff in the past, they thought they could pin this one on me? No way."

I stiffen. What's he talking about?

"Wh-what kind of stuff?" I ask, afraid to hear his response.

He pushes himself off the counter and takes a tentative step toward me.

"Nothing for you to concern your pretty little self with. Nothing to make the bastards think I'd kill a man. Good thing they had me locked up when that broad got killed, or they surely would have accused me of that one too," he says in almost a growl. "What did you say your name was?" He tilts his head.

"I didn't."

"Well, how am I supposed to get to know you, then, beautiful?"

I back up slowly toward the door, suddenly afraid and regretting my decision to rush here. Then I offer him a timid smile.

"Well, thank you for letting me stop by. I've got to go now. My friend's waiting in the car," I say, gesturing to the outside with my thumb.

"Well, she could have come in too. I don't bite. Unless you ask me to."

Okay, this guy is a weirdo. He doesn't even know me! Are the police sure he didn't do it? I can see why they thought it was him.

"Ha, ha," I fake a laugh. "Have a great day! Bye!"

I use my back to push open the door so I don't have to take my eyes off him before I walk briskly back to my car. Once I make it, I lock myself safely inside.

Chapter 30

Something that creep said to me struck a chord.

"Good thing they had me locked up when that broad got killed, or they surely would have accused me of that one too."

It made me think of the guy I had seen talking to her one day, months ago. I imagined a creepy scenario at the time, but what if it had some merit?

I mentioned him to the detectives, but did they take me seriously? The guy isn't a usual on my route, which means he isn't always in the same place at the same time. I couldn't even tell them a lot about him, so as far as the police are concerned, any young guy in the neighborhood could be a suspect. They may never find him. I'm sure lots of men live in and traverse that neighborhood, so he could easily be anybody.

But here I am now, believing myself to actually be the amateur sleuth I pretended to be just yesterday.

That dude could have killed the guy and the woman for all I know.

I decided to cruise casually in between deliveries, taking far longer than usual, in an attempt to stumble upon this guy. I don't even know if I'll recognize him if I see him, but I may as well give it a try.

Confronting strange men—not the best or safest way to

spend one's time. You'd think after yesterday I'd have learned my lesson, but nope, here I am.

Once again, I'm trying to find him without a clue about what I'll do if I succeed. When I approach the stop sign, I take a left. That was the direction I noticed them in all those weeks ago. I drive slowly. A man jogs toward me, and I slow down even more, but as he passes by, I can tell he's not the one I'm seeking. This guy has no shirt on and seems cocky, while the other one seemed more self-conscious.

When I reach the end of the street, I pull into an empty driveway to turn around. I'm not giving up yet. I'm going to keep tracing the streets of this neighborhood to see if I can find him.

I realize the odds are highly improbable, but I've learned a lot from people-watching over the past years. Humans are creatures of habit—same routine, same places, same times. It's not an exact science. Things happen that are beyond our control, but with any luck, he'll be walking the neighborhood like he was the day I saw him talking to her.

As I approach the stop sign, I see a figure in the distance, so I continue after pausing at the intersection. It's a man's back, but there's no denying that it could belong to him. The guy. The killer?

They say that the killer always returns to the scene of the crime. From what the police said, the woman was murdered nearby.

I pull the car to the side once I get within a few feet of him, and by the way his shoulders appear to stiffen, I can tell he senses me pulling over to the sidewalk.

I turn off the ignition, gently slide out of the driver's-side door, and saunter over to him so as not to spook him. The smell of my car's exhaust lingers in the air as I approach the man.

He turns around to see what's happening and pauses when he sees me walking toward him.

He looks at me, confused. If I were in his position, I'd react the same way, of course. Luckily for me, his name is embroidered on the polo he's wearing. Ryan works at a nearby mechanic shop, from the look of his clothing.

"Hey," I say.

This guy is skittish. I'm just a girl. I couldn't possibly hurt him. He has to know that, right? Sure, women are scared when guys sneak up on them, but there have been many cases of guys doing bad things. Not the other way around.

"Hi?" he asks me, the question evident in his voice.

"This is going to sound crazy"—I laugh to put him at ease—"but I've seen you around here before. You live here?"

"Yeah, down the road. Why?"

Rather than answering his question, I ask another.

"When I see you walking, where are you usually headed?"

Based on his hesitant smile and friendly stance, I can tell he wants to be nice to me, but there's no doubt he feels un-comfortable with me randomly showing up and interrogating him.

"Umm, I go to the gas station sometimes?" he asks, evidently unsure if that's the answer I'm hoping to hear.

I twist the tip of my shoe into the ground and place my arms behind me, trying to appear innocent and flirtatious, even though he's probably younger than I am, given his trendy clothing and the phone glued to his hand.

"Oh." I laugh and glance away before returning my stare and looking up at him through my eyelashes. "Sure you're not off to go see some girl?"

In an attempt to appear nervous, I suck on my top lip slightly, causing me to taste a hint of salt from the sweat that must have settled there.

He looks appalled at my accusation. He probably thinks I'm some kid's mom, and if that's how he sees me, I must seem pretty creepy.

"What's this about?" he finally asks, his hands flailing in question, no longer wanting to play my game.

I drop the act and ask him what I really want to know.

"Did you know the girl who was murdered?"

His eyes open wide.

"Who are you?"

"Concerned citizen," I say, waving my hand to indicate that's the only response he'll get to that query. "I know that you know her. I saw you two talking once."

"What are you saying?"

"I'm not saying anything. I'm asking."

"Look, I don't know what you're trying to insinuate, but you can leave me alone, psycho."

I hold up my hands in a self-protective gesture.

"I'm not insinuating anything."

I mean, that's why I'm here, but I don't need to validate his concerns.

"I just want to know if the cops know about your connection to her?"

"What connection? The one where we live in the same neighborhood?" he almost yells.

I didn't expect him to become so defensive; he looks so timid.

"Okay, I'm backing off. Sorry to have bothered you."

He rolls his eyes at me before walking away.

That went about as well as you'd expect with me going into

that encounter blind. He looked so shy and scrawny that it was hard to believe he became so aggressive so quickly. The way he acted, though, supported my theory even further. Why act like that if you've got nothing to hide?

Seems that you never truly know what some people are capable of.

Chapter 31

When I get back home and rest in my bed with the soft sheets pulled up to my chin, I hold my phone in my hand, unsure of what to do next. I'm struggling between doing the right thing and protecting myself from continued inquiries from the police.

I'll never stop wondering how I got into this mess. How I, of all the people in this town, have connections to both murders. How do I, an almost middle-aged single woman, a normal woman, get stuck in a position like this?

This isn't supposed to happen to people like me. Isn't this more fitting for a drug dealer or gambling addict? Individuals who already tend to participate in unsavory situations?

Ignore the fact that I was inside someone's home without their consent. That's small potatoes in the grand scheme of everything. Which leads me to my latest conundrum, not to be confused with any of the others, although all my problems lately involve murder, much to my dismay.

I could tell the police about that young man, Ryan. I found him, after all. I know where he goes every day, so they can surely use that information to identify and question him. The way he acted was so obviously defensive. I can't help but think he knows something about the murder, or could even have been involved.

What is with my new proclivity for danger?

On the one hand, I can tell the police that I found the guy. Reiterate that I've seen him talking to the victim near her home. I could say I'd seen him lingering around the scene of the crime, although it would be a small white lie. He lives there, so he *can't* avoid being near the scene of the crime. It isn't much; hell, it isn't even really incriminating, but they're desperate for information, so they'd at least look into it. Ideally, they'd interrogate him and he'd confess. Then I could say I'd done my civic duty and allowed the victim's family the ability to seek justice.

But I must also consider the other possibilities that are associated with reporting what I know to the police. Maybe it's my anxiety, but I always formulate worst-case scenarios as well. Let's say they question him and it leads nowhere; then I've gone and put myself back on their radar. As I've said, they're desperate, so they're looking to put the blame on anyone that they can.

What if they find it suspicious that I continue randomly recalling seemingly vital information after they've already asked me? What if they begin to target me? Once I'm a suspect of interest, they'll require me to provide a DNA sample. I may very well be a match for the hair found at the first crime scene. That would be the nail in my coffin.

So what, I report him? Try to do the right thing for one murder victim, only to be convicted of another murder myself?

That idea helps to solidify my decision, or at least encourages me to hold off on telling the police what I know. I've waited this long to tell them about him, so what's a little while longer?

I'm about to put my phone down on my bedside table, but

before I do, I change my mind and open the texts between Lucas and me, and I can't keep the smile off my face.

We picked up right where we left off, like years haven't gone by since the last time we spoke. He's always so complimentary and cute with his good-morning texts and goofy side notes about his day. I love that we don't have to mess around, pretend, and play games with each other. We're so comfortable with one another that we've jumped seamlessly into a full relationship at the drop of a hat.

If I want to talk to him, I just pull out my phone, and I do. I missed being able to tell him every little thing about my day. I missed how he showered me with compliments. I missed hearing the distinct notification sound that indicated it was him and not anyone else.

I don't feel the worry that you usually feel with new relationships. Not wanting to text too much and be a bother or seem too eager. Hesitant to say things that may get taken the wrong way. Not with Lucas.

I am simply my genuine, authentic self, and the best part about it... he accepts me as I am, and I love him for who he is. We're already comfortable with each other, and it's so nice to skip that awkward phase of a relationship and go straight into just being there for one another.

Now, I'd hope he would still feel the same if I told him all the mental fatigue I'd been experiencing since the first murder. I'm not totally sure he would, though. I know him well, and I want to say that he'd understand, but he might not. I'd feel so much better if I could unload all this baggage on someone instead of having internal conversations all the time.

I shake the thought from my head. I can't tell him anything yet. I can't ruin what we've just started so soon. I can't fathom losing one of the few things in my life that brings me ineffable joy. I can't risk confessing in the hopes that he'll accept me, only for him to shun me instead.

There's no denying my presence at the scene of the first murder is sketchy. It looks bad! I get it. I understand it too well, and that's why I hide it away. That's why I worry. It doesn't look good. If I don't think it looks good and I know the truth... imagine how someone who wasn't there would see it.

So I have to go on. Forgetting. Refusing to acknowledge it. I have to continue living with this unexplainable guilt and these raging thoughts. I cannot burden anyone else. I just long for the day when it's all in the past and what is likely the worst part of my life is done and resolved.

My phone chimes then—not with just any sound but my favorite one.

Loo-Kiss: *Goodnight, gorgeous. I'll be dreaming of you.*

My cheeks flush, and I squeeze my eyes shut, trying to contain the affection I feel so I can allow it to guide me into a peaceful sleep.

Chapter 32

I've always enjoyed watching others. It's a guilty pleasure of mine. Sometimes I overstep. I move past the innocent line of curiosity. I do things I know I shouldn't. I venture into obsession. The desire fueling my every move, causing my body to react and for goose bumps to ripple on my flesh. Once I do, there's no turning back. I know this about myself, and I've come to accept it.

Sure, I can try not to. I have willed myself to slow down, even to pause, but it cannot be stopped. No, I can only hold back this monster inside for so long until it escapes the prison I've constructed for it. I really do try to hold it at bay and lock the sinful thoughts away. I've been successful but never for long.

I hoped that by ignoring it and pushing it to the back, it would stay there. I was unsure how to truly extinguish my unorthodox desires. The monster always finds a way to hammer at the barrier until nothing is left to keep it confined. No, this monster cannot be defeated, only suppressed.

This unruly, obsessive part of my soul escapes, no matter the effort I put in to keep it contained. I've come to relish those moments, though. The moment that the urge becomes so strong that I can almost imagine steel bars bending beneath the pressure, no match for the power of my desires.

Those moments are the ones in which I do things that I never thought I'd do.

Like now, I'm unable to stay away any longer. I cherish the time I'm able to watch her sleep, her blond hair matted on the side of her head from where she probably began her journey into the dream world. Her oversized T-shirt covering her to her mid-thigh, the right sleeve bunched up to her shoulder from tossing in her sleep. I understand the depravity of what I'm doing, but I've gotten to the point where my deep-seated malicious conquest has become inevitable.

The camera? Ha, nice try. I placed my camera first, and she didn't find it during her initial search. Thank the heavens for small favors.

Mine doesn't see into her bedroom, though. So occasionally, I have to sneak inside undetected. A pick-me-up, an appetizer, really, to keep me going. To fuel my fire. For moments when I am unable to keep the cage closed.

I want to believe she's clueless, but the way she's been acting, paired with the installation of the camera, tells me she's onto something.

She might have forced my hand. I'd have enjoyed this part longer. The part of my game where she's unaware of my entrance into her life as my presence rolls in like storm clouds, all the while masquerading as relief from drought, rather than the terrifying thunderstorm that I am.

I enjoy the first stages of my descent into obsession much more, the part where she feels safe and goes about her normal routine. That way, I get to see the real Zoey. The part of her that no one gets to see.

That step is now tarnished. She's aware, yet still clueless.

She doesn't know what I have in store for her. She doesn't see the future for her that I've laid out.

I walk like a chameleon amongst others, never allowing anyone to see me at my core. I hide it so well that I almost don't have to try. After all, the darkness doesn't feel like me, just a part of me. It's not my fault because I don't want to have urges like this; who does? I crave normalcy and parade my innocence when I can.

I can put the monster back in the cage; I have before, and I will try again. I always try. Sadly, my mere mortal body is no match for the insidious part of my soul.

Chapter 33

In keeping with my promise to see my friends more often, I asked Kaci, Sierra, and Bianca to meet me at the Loony Bin for drinks. As I walk through the glass doors, I see the trio has already beaten me here and is nestled in a booth toward the back of the room.

I rush over to my friends, happy for the distraction they can offer.

They let out a cumulative rumble of cheers as they see me approach. The table is already littered with alcoholic beverages, and I see one of my friends has already ordered me a mango margarita, which sits in front of the empty space remaining in the booth.

"Awww," I say as I take my seat. "You guys ordered my drink for me? Y'all are too sweet!"

"Yes, girl! We're celebrating!"

"We are? Celebrating what?" I ask.

Sierra raises a glass that currently houses a nearly empty violet cocktail, the condensation falling slowly.

I'm in mid-sip, savoring the tangy treat as the cold liquid travels down my throat, when she explains.

"The Southern Slasher has officially been confirmed as the killer of that poor girl Abby."

'That's good because..." I pause, allowing my companions to fill in the blanks for me.

Bianca clears her throat and straightens up in the seat opposite mine.

"Well, as your local police liaison, I am here to confirm that we have found evidence at the second crime scene to confirm the victim was indeed killed by the Southern Slasher. We also know he—"

"Or she," Kaci interrupts.

"Or she," Bianca says, directing a stare toward Kaci before continuing, "only kills one person a year. So, with that being said, it's assumed we are safe and no longer have to fear for our lives!"

It feels so morbid to find pleasure at the expense of an innocent woman's life, but Bianca's right. If the killer adheres to his own set of rules, we are safe.

I interrupt my friends' cheers of joy.

"What about the other guy, Alan?"

They all become silent, unsure of what to say.

"Someone killed him. We still can't be sure that we're safe. They let that creep off the hook, so he's just out there running loose. How do we know if we'll ever be safe again? How do we know who we can trust?" I say, making sure I look each of them in the eye.

"Okay," Kaci says, breaking the silence. "Since when did you become the pessimist of the group?"

I heave an audible sigh.

"I get it. I want to feel safe too. I'm sorry that I see it this way, but I do. Yes, they know it's the Southern Slasher, but they don't even know who he is? So there's no justice for her. For him..." I pause, trying to find the words. "We don't know who killed him either. So really, what's good about that?"

I've stunned them. Heck, I've even caught myself off guard. Obviously, I feel such remorse about the whole thing, but they're experiencing it differently. They didn't know the guy. *They* didn't discover his body.

"I mean... what if the first guy was supposed to be the serial killer's victim?" Sierra says timidly, pursing her lips to the side. "What if he or she"—now she looks at Kaci—"got startled or something caught him or her off guard so they couldn't finish their ritual?" She makes air quotes with her fingers when she says "ritual."

I stop and consider that, looking around to learn what everyone else thinks, and I see Kaci and Bianca nod.

Bianca chimes in, "Really, that makes sense. The Southern Slasher has a distinguished and established MO. I mean, he is a serial killer, after all. If he couldn't finish what he set out to do... if he was interrupted or spooked, then of course he'd flee to evade capture. It wouldn't be worth getting caught to stay around and finish."

Wow, maybe that was what happened. Maybe I interrupted him, kind of like he interrupted me. We both chose the same time to be in the house, although for different purposes. He didn't expect me to be there, and I didn't expect him to be there.

Her reasoning makes sense, and if she's correct, it means that we're safe for now. The relief is palpable, and tension begins to fall from my body, causing me to feel lighter and straighten up in my seat.

I choose that moment to take a long sip from my drink, and I look up to find my companions all staring at me.

I shrug.

"When you put it like that...." I say, trailing off and lifting my glass, "maybe we *can* celebrate."

Chapter 34

A few hours later, I pull into the driveway with a euphoric sensation. Not from the alcohol, even though I can still sense it on my tongue, but from the changes that are shifting in my favor.

Lucas and I are together again, I have my friends back for good as well as a job I love, and best of all, I can finally begin to put this horrendous chapter of my life behind me.

Sure, my thoughts aren't completely calm. I'm still me, and that's not changing anytime soon. My brain continues to throw what-ifs at me.

What if the Southern Slasher knows it was me? What if they put my name on their hit list? What if the police ever come around asking for a sample of my DNA?

But those thoughts — those are minuscule and, in my opinion, very unlikely.

The Southern Slasher has an MO, and I don't know how he chooses his victims, but for my peace of mind, I have to think it's at random. Ideally, he ran when he heard me. Ideally, he never saw me. Ideally, he doesn't know who I am.

Well, there are the notes... but I haven't received a new one recently, and if he sent them, maybe he just wanted to spook me? That sounds like something a serial killer would enjoy:

striking immeasurable fear into a woman.

He might very well have run. Hell, that's what I did. I found that man's body and hightailed my way out of there, afraid of getting caught.

With that hair, well, I've got to be so far down on the police's radar that they probably won't ever talk to me again, especially if they pin the murders on the Southern Slasher.

Bianca told me she'd been paying attention to where the officers met to discuss the murders and the case in general ever since the day they asked me to go to the station. Earlier, she told me that, from what she could see, I wasn't on a suspect list or brought up in any of their conversations.

I practically float to my door and unlock it with ease. The cool air welcomes me in from the heat and humidity of the night.

The camera snags my attention, and I realize that I absent-mindedly let a couple of days lapse in between checking the footage.

I probably don't even need it anymore. Well, I don't want to need it, but whether I do has yet to be determined.

I place my purse down in the kitchen, make my way to my favorite spot on the couch, and fall into the worn indention.

I should probably shower first, but now that the camera is on my mind, I can't stop thinking about it. I need to see that nothing's on there to really confirm that I am safe and can begin to relax.

I kick off my shoes and pull my legs underneath me as I pull up the app that lets me review the camera footage.

At first, it's boring watching my very still house when I'm not home. Initially, I watch the footage as is, but I realize if I continue to do that, I'll be here all night, so I decide to speed up the video.

Nothing moves except dust particles here and there. When I see movement, I slow the footage down again only to look at the time stamp and realize it's displaying when I typically get home from work.

I watch myself come home and flit around the house. I hate seeing myself on camera just as much as I hate hearing my voice on a recording, so I speed up the footage again. I'm home and I'm awake, so I know nothing will happen.

This video is from a few days ago, and I can't remember when I went to bed that evening, but after I've been gone from the screen for a while, I speed up the footage once more. I don't speed it up too fast, though, afraid to miss something. Gosh, I don't want to see anything at night. Talk about new fears being unlocked.

I scroll through the video, and the time stamp is at 3:00 a.m. when I see movement in the periphery of the camera. I slam my finger down on the pause button. Something is moving just outside the angle of the camera, but it's so blurry and fast that I can't tell what it is.

More dust? I can't blame it on a pet, since I have none. I also know I wasn't awake at three o'clock in the morning. There's a bathroom in my bedroom, and I keep a bottle of water on my bedside table, so I never leave my bedroom at night.

I hit Play again. I need to see if the shadow moves into view of the camera. It doesn't. It's gone just as quickly as it appeared. I slow the speed and watch until the time I usually wake up to see if I can spot the shadow again, but it never comes back.

That's good, right? If it were a person, it would have to leave the same way it came. But in that case, the person wouldn't know the camera was there in the dark. Right? They shouldn't know that it's there and therefore wouldn't know to avoid it.

Odds were it was just a bug that got in or a puff of dust.

I speed through the footage again, watching as I leave for work the next day to when I get back home.

When the footage progresses to another nightfall, I slow the video down a little, hoping to see, or avoid seeing, that shadow again.

The time stamp shows 1:37 a.m. the next time I see movement, and I slam down my finger again to pause the video. I stare at the shadow again, and I see more of it is visible this time. That's the outline of a person. I'm sure of it. God, I don't want to press Play, but I must.

First, though, I look up at the camera on the entertainment center. There's no light to indicate that the device is recording, and I'm sure that it gets too dark in here at night for anyone to know it's perched there.

After that, I look at the space in my living room beyond the camera's scope—the same spot that this shadow crossed at an ungodly time of night—and a shiver runs down my spine.

How could anyone get into my house without me knowing? There are no scratches or broken locks on the doors or windows—at least, not that I've noticed. Could they have a key? How on earth would they have gotten a key to my house?

Just minutes ago, I was convincing myself that I was safe, but I was so wrong.

I press Play. I've got to know what's going on so that I can prepare myself for tonight. Jesus, that's if I can even stay here. I'm so frightened by the shadowy figure in the footage that there's no way I'm staying home tonight.

The video continues, as do my thoughts, and the person that I see enter the frame makes my jaw drop and my thoughts cease. I'd recognize that hair anywhere.

Chapter 35

I can't believe my eyes as I watch the woman in the video walk from my bedroom to the kitchen. Just as she reaches the threshold between the living room and the kitchen, she pauses and doesn't move. She stares into the kitchen for five minutes before she finally turns around and faces the camera.

It's me.

My eyes are open, but I look tired and almost lifeless. I never get up in the middle of the night. I never leave my room, since I have everything I need there.

Why am I roaming the house during the night? Why don't I remember waking up?

Unless I'm not awake. In the video, I hardly look like myself. Even my posture is different from its appearance in the earlier footage of me flitting around the house after work. I know I don't have good posture in general: I genuinely slouch all the time. But not in this video. My back is ramrod straight, and there's not one single indication of my feelings or thoughts evident on my face.

I must have been sleepwalking. I've never done that before. I don't know much about it, but surely it's possible. It has to be; it's the only thing that makes sense.

The footage has no sound, but I can't imagine I'd hear

anything if it did. All I can hear is my pulse reverberating through my skull as I watch in confusion.

I minimize the app, the glass screen warm against my fingertip, and pull up a search engine on my phone. Sure enough, if the internet is to be believed, you can apparently start sleepwalking out of nowhere. I skim the sentences on the Web page I've clicked on, my eyes darting rapidly back and forth:

Also known as somnambulism, sleepwalking is characterized by individuals who are able to perform complex activities while asleep. Usually occurring during non-REM sleep, sleepwalking typically happens in the first part of the night as the sleep cycle begins. Sleepwalking is usually seen in children but can occur in adults as well. Sleepwalking may be a result of genetics, medications, or underlying medical conditions. Symptoms can also be triggered by high levels of stress and anxiety.

DING DING DING. We have a winner.

I've definitely been under a lot of stress lately. Anxiety? Always. So I'm sleepwalking. Wow, I didn't even realize it. I wonder for how long? Jesus, was I the one who moved that dang clock? In my sleep?

Wait a minute. The things moving around the house can probably be explained by my newly appointed diagnosis. I'm not a doctor, but there's no denying all the signs are there.

I close out the Web page, open the camera app back up, and resume the video. I watch myself pace throughout the house slowly, occasionally picking up items, holding them for way too long and for no reason at all, before placing them down again.

There's no rhyme or reason to what I'm doing, what I touch, and for how long I do it. It's all so very random and unpredictable. At one point, I held the TV remote for a solid twenty minutes just to put it back where I got it.

Luckily, I don't appear to sleepwalk for too long. In the footage, I head back toward my room when the timestamp shows 2:26 a.m. I hope I go straight back to bed instead of wandering around aimlessly in my room. Maybe that was why my slipper was under my bed the other day.

No wonder I've been so tired lately. I'm so stressed that I can hardly sleep, and when I do, I'm sleepwalking and not even getting a solid night's rest!

I fast-forward to the next night and, sure enough, I'm at it again at 12:57 a.m., walking around the house like a zombie, touching and moving objects for no reason at all, before retreating to my bedroom.

To think that if I didn't set this camera up, I might never have known.

Well, I guess I don't have to be scared to be here anymore, now that I've proven the one moving the items wasn't a stranger but just zonked-out me.

I wonder if I'll stop doing it now that my guilty conscience will start to recede alongside my stress levels?

If I've been doing this without knowing... who's to say I haven't committed any other sinister actions without know-ing?

My speculative thoughts know no bounds.

Suddenly, a scene begins to unfold in my mind. No, not a scene but a memory:

I'm in the first murder victim's house. I exit the last room that I've been exploring only to be startled by him. The homeowner is there, standing in the living room. Surprise and shock settle on his face as he takes a defensive stance.

I put my arms up, trying to show him I mean no harm to him. Oh man, I'm screwed. He's going to call the police.

"What are you doing here?" he asks me, but I can't answer.

"Who are you?" he asks when I don't reply to his first inquiry.

I'm not telling him who I am. Absolutely not. I'll lose my job. I'll be arrested. My life will be over, and I'll never be able to get another job. No one will hire me. I'll lose all the money I have defending myself only to still be found guilty. I'll lose my house. No one will trust me. My friends will never support me. I'll be homeless.

I begin to shake as the reality of it all crashes down on me.

He goes to grab his phone from his pocket.

"No, wait," I barely manage to squeak.

"Look, lady. I don't know who you are or what you're doing here, but I know that you have no right to be here. I'm calling the police. So stay right there," he says to me, throwing his hand out in front of him, willing me to stay still and wait for the cops to come.

In that moment, I don't fight, I don't freeze; instead I surprise myself and I take flight. I try to make a run for the door, but he jerks back, perhaps thinking I'm going to attack him.

He speeds toward his kitchen, probably trying to grab a knife, but I'll be long gone by the time he gets ahold of one. I'm just about to make it to the door when I hear a sickening thud.

I freeze just as I'm about to slip out of the open door; the man must have left it ajar when he came home.

I turn to look, not sure what I'll find. Oh God, he's dead, and it's all because of me.

Chapter 36

No wonder I feel so guilty. It's because I am guilty. I didn't mean for him to die. I didn't even try to hurt him, but that doesn't matter. He's dead because of me.

My stupid mind has been both protecting and tormenting me all this time. If I hadn't been there, or hell, if I had let him call 911, he'd still be alive. A whole human, a person, a good man could still be living and breathing if it weren't for me and my stupid hobby.

My absurd and irrational hobby! I never thought it could be harmful. It was always just the ideal way to feed my curiosity and blow off steam. Sure, it wasn't innocent, but jeez, it wasn't necessarily dangerous either. I was always so careful.

There's no denying it now. I see it clearly in my head. The scene is on repeat now. I notice small details change sometimes; for example, his socks are usually white, but sometimes I observe that they're black, or his hair is parted in a different way, or the stance he takes once I come out of his bedroom has altered.

It's probably because I'm tormenting myself, playing the event over and over again in my head.

I keep thinking about it because I don't understand. Initially, I remembered coming out of the room and finding his body.

Did I create that memory falsely? Did my brain do that to try to protect me from the truth, only to fail miserably?

Obviously, something isn't right. I've felt guilty this whole time, and now I understand why. I'm sleepwalking, which I've never done before, on top of my obsession with being so dang curious.

Maybe I've finally cracked. What if it gets worse? What if with each passing day, I lose more and more of myself and, as a result, everything that I care about?

Although the temperature in the room is cool, I feel sweat begin to bead on my forehead. My right leg bounces uncontrollably as thoughts ricochet in my brain.

I should turn myself in. I can tell the police everything, and although I know I'll have to be in prison for some time, maybe once they understand the fragility of my mind, they'll evaluate me and get me the help I need.

As guilty as I feel, that underlying message still flashes into my mind intermittently: *It wasn't intentional.*

Do I deserve to be sentenced to prison for a murder I didn't intend to commit? Maybe I can confess and they'll realize that the crime scene does appear accidental and just charge me with trespassing? There's no way to tell what they'll believe, what they'll charge me with, how long I'll be in prison, and if the authorities will even factor my mental instability into the equation.

I may not know what will happen from here if I decide to confess, but I know someone who might. I know it's late, but just to confirm, I look at the clock, which shows the time to be past midnight.

I can't wait until tomorrow. I can't live like this anymore. Not now that I know the truth, not now that I remember it.

I call Bianca, and just as the phone rings for the sixth time and I'm debating what to do next if she doesn't answer, I hear her utter a sleepy "Hello?"

"B, I need you. Can you come over?"

There's a pause, since I'm sure she's looking at the time and considering her answer.

"Sure. If you wanted to have a sleepover, you could have said so earlier."

I let out a laugh that turns quickly into a cry.

"Aw, hold on, Z. I'll be right there."

She hangs up, and I unlock the door for her so that she can come in whenever she gets here.

Bianca works for the police! The police! I'm basically signing up to be convicted if I tell her anything, that much is for sure.

I've been struggling with this all by myself, and a fat lot of good it's done me. I need to tell someone. I need to hear someone else's opinions, someone else's thoughts. I'm sick of talking to myself.

I'm absolutely terrified of what Bianca will think. Once I confess, she'll never see me the same way again. She'll disown me, too ashamed to keep me as a friend. I just know she'll feel betrayed that I've kept things from her. How can she trust me again once she finds out that I've been lying to her face? At least she should be able to tell me what the authorities are likely to charge me with and prepare me for my arrest.

Regardless of the repercussions, my mind is made up. It's too late to change it now.

That thought is confirmed further when I hear a light knock at the door. I turn to see Bianca ease her way in the door upon realizing that I left it unlocked for her.

Her hair is messy, and she's still in her pajama set: a neon pink tank top and a pair of matching sleep shorts. I'm nearly sure that I woke her up, but she looks wide awake, concern in her eyes as she approaches me on the couch.

She takes a moment to stare at me, likely noticing I'm still in the denim shorts and short-sleeved blouse I wore earlier tonight. She's also probably observing what I'm sure is streaked mascara running down my face. As she sits beside me, I don't move, remaining in an upright fetal position, my legs pulled into my chest.

"What's wrong?"

I don't know how to talk about it. I don't know where to start. So I just spit out the first response I think of and decide to go from there.

"I need your help."

"Okay. Talk to me."

"I don't know what to do," I mumble before looking up to make eye contact with her.

"Breathe," she says as she performs an exaggerated exhalation, and I feel the whoosh of air graze my bare knee.

I do as she says, inhaling through my nose and pushing out a large breath.

Then I begin to laugh hysterically.

"I don't know where to start. I guess I need to start at the beginning."

She nods, and I look away, giving her the chance to process what I have to say without me analyzing her facial expressions. It's not merely for her but for me too. I can't bear to see the disgust on her face as I confess my sins to her. So instead, I tuck my chin and look down at my knees.

"It sounds crazy, but sometimes I like to go into strangers' homes. I always go when no one is home, and I don't ever do it with ill intent. One day I just realized how interesting it would be to see the figurative skeletons people hide in their literal closets."

I look at her out of the corner of my eye and see a sympathetic expression on her face, and I'm glad she isn't trying to ask me questions.

I shake my head, unsure of how to say the next part—the hardest part.

"I was at Alan's house the day he died. I was digging around and was just about to leave when he caught me. I was terrified of getting into trouble. I always thought I'd be the type to freeze, but I wasn't. I ran for the door, hoping to get away before he could identify me or my car, or before the cops would come. I don't know if he thought I was going to hurt him, or what, but he went to the kitchen, and right before I made it out the door, he fell. God, I don't think I can get that sound out of my head. The *thunk* as his head hit the floor." I grimace.

"Actually, for a long time, my brain hid that part from me, until tonight, that is. This whole time, I thought that I had stumbled upon his body, and I ran away without calling the cops because I didn't want to get in trouble for being there when I shouldn't have been. That was bad enough. I felt guilty, but I kept telling myself there was nothing I could have done to save him. But I was wrong. If I hadn't been there, he'd still be alive."

The seriousness of what I've done sets in then, and I start to cry, hiding my face in the alcove between my legs and chest. Not only that, but I cry with the relief of having shared this secret with someone, and I cry in fear, too, worried about what my best friend will think of me.

Chapter 37

"I know you."

At those words, I look up at Bianca through my tears. She's said them so softly that I'm not sure that I've heard her right.

Then she smiles at me and says our little inside joke like she usually does, mocking me from when I said it all those years ago.

"You know me!"

I laugh through my sobs.

"I do know you. I know your favorite color. I know how you daydream. I know that you're kind. I even know that your mom kept using that juice pitcher even after you chased a hamster around with it." She pauses, giving me a look of disgust. Then she continues, "I also know you wouldn't intentionally hurt anyone. What I don't know is why you didn't tell me you were going through this sooner."

"I couldn't. I didn't want you to look at me differently."

"Look at me," she says, pointing at her face. "Does it look like I'm looking at you differently? No, I'm not."

"Oh, come on. Do you think if the roles were reversed, you'd act differently?"

She purses her lips as she considers what I've said.

"Maybe you're right. But now that I do know, I wish I had

known sooner. I wish I could've helped. Man, I could have even followed the case closer and informed you about things with more consideration for your mental health."

She wrinkles her brows as she looks around the room.

"I feel bad now," she says. "The way I talked about it so openly, not knowing just how invested you were in everything I had to say about it."

"Wait a minute," I reply as the realization sets in. "You're not scared of me? You're not going to turn me in?"

"I mean, I can see it from your point of view. You did nothing wrong."

That she says my mantra back to me without knowing how much it means to me fills me with solace.

After the return of those memories and the guilt I've felt for weeks, I finally confess and she absolves me immediately? Would everyone see it like that, or would only she see it that way because we'd been friends for so long?

"You say that. Not everyone will see it like that."

She nods.

"You're right. Unfortunately, they don't know you like I do. I know how desperate they are to convict someone of murder. There's no denying that the family wants justice."

Just then, her eyes widen, and she stares at my hair.

"Zoey, is there a possibility that the hair they have in evidence is yours?"

She doesn't need to ask, and I don't have to answer. I can tell by the furrow in her brow and the serious expression on her face that she knows the answer.

I grimace and shrug.

"It could be. That's another reason I've been so out of it lately. I'm terrified."

"Okay, okay. Let me think."

I do just that. I have no idea what's going through her head, but maybe if I did, I could offer her some advice. I keep quiet instead, not willing to break her shut-eyed look of concentration.

"I can get rid of your hair."

Her sudden statement cuts viciously through the silence. The idea sounds too good to be true. She just destroys evidence? It can't be that easy. I can't allow her to risk her job for me. I'm the one who's done something wrong. I never wanted to involve her like this.

"You can't."

I don't even know what I mean when I say it.

I know that if she's said that she can, she probably thinks that she is capable, although it won't be easy. I don't want her to put her career at risk for me.

"I can. I will. You did not intentionally hurt that man. You shouldn't have to worry for the rest of your life. You shouldn't have to live in fear that you'll be convicted of a crime you didn't commit."

"But—"

"But nothing," she interrupts me before I can continue, causing me to pause. "There's not a thing you could say to change my mind about this. I am doing it. Now sit there and listen while I brainstorm aloud," she says, looking at me to ensure I'll obey her.

I nod.

"The hair was analyzed, and the data is cataloged electronically. With technology being what it is today, I imagine it'll be nearly impossible to erase the genetic profile data obtained from the hair. Maybe if we knew some kind of crazy hacker genius, we could get rid of that, but that only happens in the movies," she says, looking at me again to see if I'm listening to her.

I nod so she knows I understand, but really, that bit on its own sounds like a nail in my coffin. I don't bother to say anything.

"The actual hair sample, though—well, that is kept in evidence, and I have no doubt that I can easily get my hands on it and destroy it for good. The DNA will still be in the computer, though if they ever connect it to you, they would need to show it in court. When they go to gather the evidence, they'll find it missing, and it should be deemed inadmissible in court," she says, tapping her chin with her index finger.

"I'd do an internet search to make sure that I'm right about that, but I don't want to leave a trail that can lead them to me. For now, we'll have to hope that I'm right. Actually, one of the podcasts I listen to, *Crimes and Crocheting*, talked about a case once that lost the evidence and it got thrown out. I think I'm right about that."

I stare at her with concern, and she must know what I'm feeling because she quickly adds, "I'll be okay! Small-town police station, remember? I can do it, and I'm positive no one will ever suspect it was an inside job. They'll chalk it up to a rookie mistake and accept defeat."

"They won't stop looking for the murderer, though," I add hesitantly.

I've accepted her plan to destroy evidence, against my better judgment, but the strategy still doesn't sound foolproof.

"Look, it isn't the best solution, but it's all we've got for now," she says as if reading my thoughts. Twirling her hair absentmindedly between her fingers, she adds, "You know, what Sierra said earlier tonight makes sense. If she's thinking that the first murder could have been a botched attempt by the Southern Slasher, then so might everyone else."

"Yes. Before I remembered what actually happened, what she said made a lot of sense," I agree.

"Let's hope that the rumor catches on and the media picks it up and starts to spread the word. Let's face it, life will never be the same, but every day will get a little easier. Besides, we have each other." With a sympathetic smile on her face, she concludes, "I know you're always there for me, and I'll do anything for you," as she reaches toward me and pats my hand gently.

How did I ever get so lucky to have a friend like Bianca?

Chapter 38

I know it must be late, but I don't even bother to look at the clock. After everything that's unfolded tonight, I know neither Bianca nor I will be able to sleep anytime soon.

I listen as Bianca reassures me of her plan to destroy my hair from evidence. The notion sounds solid. She's right about one thing. We live in a small town, and we don't see a lot of murders or crime, so I think the hair going missing can easily be explained away by inexperienced investigators. I don't love the thought of the backlash they'll get for losing evidence, but add it to the list of things I'm forced to live with, and it doesn't seem that bad.

Speaking with Bianca has softened my fears but only slightly. I'm not sure I'll ever get over what I've done, no matter how much she may attempt to reassure me of my innocence. There's no doubt in my mind that if I didn't have this disgusting habit of invading people's private property, the man would still be alive. That fact alone makes me guilty. It will be a guilt with which I'll learn to live.

I'll make up for it. I'll stop this monster inside me. Right now, at this very moment, I vow to no longer dig into strangers' things. I'll just have to find another way to satiate my inherent hunger for drama. I'll find a way to curb my obsession.

I'll even start contributing more to the community. I've got to make up for what I've taken away. I can join in community cleanups, volunteer at local events, and participate in worthy organizations. When you think about it, I have the time.

That's if I can pull myself away from Lucas.

Oh, Lucas.

Can I ever tell him what I've done? Will he notice that I'm not the same person I used to be? If I tell him, will it change the way he feels about me?

Why am I always such a mess? I always overanalyze everything.

I look over at Bianca as she sits next to me. We are both lost in our thoughts.

She turns to look at me, a blank stare in her eyes, as she senses my glance in her direction.

Something in her expression scares me. She's usually so cheerful and bright, but right now, she looks expressionless. Her dead eyes are focused on me, but I feel as if she is looking through me and not at me.

Concern swells in my chest. Oh, no. She's thought about it. Time has passed, and as we've sat in silence, she's decided I'm not worth the risk. I can tell by her face, devoid of emotion, that she has begun to regret her decision. She's scared of me.

"Bianca," I say, but I don't know what else to say. I can't change her mind. I'm surprised she even went along with my nonsense in the first place. I should have known better.

Hearing her name pulls her from her trance. Her vacant stare turns quickly into a lackluster smile.

"Sorry. I was thinking. Can I tell you something?"

"Of course." I stare at her, eyebrows raised. "Obviously."

There's nothing I can do. She's been sitting with her

thoughts, and all I can do at this point is listen to her.

"I have a secret of my own to confess, and I hope that you'll be understanding," she tells me hesitantly.

My curiosity is piqued, although that doesn't take much. I sit up and turn to face her, giving her the respect she deserves. I want her to know she has my full attention and that I care about what she has to say. It's not a charade, and I don't have to pretend to care just to make sure she doesn't change her mind about helping me. I care about her.

She laughs, but the sound isn't joyful. It seems brooding. I watch the corners of her eyes wrinkle slightly as she does.

"Wow. I don't know how to say it," she says as she looks at me. She begins to shake her head before continuing.

"The second victim, the woman... Well, when the first murder occurred, she called in a tip. I answered the phone that day, just like I always do. She sounded flustered when I asked her name, and instead she insisted that she wanted to remain anonymous. I told her that I still needed her name to put on file, but it wouldn't be made public. It was her, Abby Roberts. She wanted to call in with some information. She saw you at the house," she says, looking up at me through her eyelashes.

My jaw drops, and I continue to listen in rapt attention.

"She didn't sound too sure of herself, and actually, she didn't know it was *you-you*, you know? I could tell, though. She was able to provide a description of your car and what you looked like. I hoped it was someone else; surely, you can't be the only blond that drives a blue SUV in town.

"She even laughed nervously over the phone. I remember it so vividly. I asked her if she knew who you were, but she said no, so I couldn't know for sure if it was you. I told her I'd relay the information to the detectives and thanked her. I thought that was it. I didn't tell the detectives, though," she says as she places a reassuring hand on my knee.

"Just in case, by some weird coincidence, it was you, I didn't pass the information on. But time went by, and she called again to inquire if we'd been able to identify the woman she saw. I recognized her voice when I answered. She told me that she had additional information that might lead us to you. 'Coffee Beams is the company she works for,' she told me with pride. 'Surely,' she explained to me, 'that's enough information for you to find her. I'm positive she had something to do with it the more I think about it,' she told me over the phone." Bianca pauses briefly, maybe to allow me to comment, but I'm too shocked to contribute to the conversation.

"I didn't know what to do. She was so confident you were guilty of something, but she was the only one who knew about you. I hadn't heard your name come up at all. Surely if you were involved, I'd have known. That day, after work, I wound up at her house and showed her your picture, hoping for her to say that it wasn't you she had recognized after all. She did the exact opposite. Her eyes lit up with recognition, and she emphatically claimed it was you and told me we had to arrest you immediately. I gawked at her, and I think she sensed my hesitation. She threatened that she'd get me fired and yelled at me, saying that we both would go to jail.

"Zoey, I had to kill her. It was a rash decision, I know, but I couldn't have her falsely incriminating you. I couldn't have her insulting my integrity and threatening my job. You have to know—at first, I thought I'd just talk to her, but once I met her, it all got out of control. I let the anger get the best of me, and I did what I felt like I had to do in the moment," she says, appearing lost in retelling her story.

I'm glad because I'm sure the face that I'm making is not comforting. I attempt to mask my emotions so as not to distract her. My stomach is in knots as she tells her story. A clammy feeling begins to spread down my neck.

"Afterwards, I sat there and thought about it. I was very careful, and I'm sure that no one saw me and that I didn't leave any evidence behind. That wasn't enough, though. I couldn't risk their thinking you or I had anything to do with her murder. Luckily, I'd been in the loop about a lot of things with the first murder, and I knew things that the public didn't know about the Southern Slasher. So I used what I knew about him to frame him for her murder. That way, they could blame it on him and not us! As you know, it seems to have worked, and I have convinced them!"

She smiles at me, and it's unsettling. Her unnerving grin seems to seep into my skin as goose bumps start to break out across my arms.

"Don't you see? I'm just like you. We both did something we shouldn't have, but it'll be okay, because we both have each other."

Chapter 39

Following Bianca's revelation last night, we hugged each other and cried. After she left in the early hours of the morning, I sat with my thoughts.

Once again, I felt as if I could not possibly go into work between the lack of sleep and all the thoughts swarming in my head. I texted Kristi around three and told her I'd been vomiting all night and couldn't go in. To me, the excuse sounded plausible. What other reason would I have to be up at three a.m.? Well, I highly doubted she'd guess I was lying so that I could soak at home in self-doubt and ponder revelations of murder. No, a stomach bug sounded good enough.

Initially, when Bianca confessed, I thought she was crazy. Admittedly, while everything she told me was outlandish, at the same time, it all made sense. It's not that I ever doubted her, which might make *me* crazy. I just couldn't believe that she cared about me so much that she'd go to such great lengths to protect me.

That part was wild. I guess it makes me a bad friend, but to be honest, I don't know if I could have done the same for her. Let's hope I never have to find out.

There's no denying that what she did is *crazy*. Murder is a sin. I don't agree with what she did, but that doesn't mean I can change it. I can't go back in time. I know there are quite a few things that I'd change if I could.

What's done is done. I know that, and I came to terms with it as we sat in silence before she confessed. So how can I judge and crucify her, while I sit in the opposing corner, essentially having committed the same crime as her?

Sure, what I did wasn't intentional, but if she's to be believed, what she did wasn't intentional either. Although I must admit that my case seems much more innocent than hers.

Wow, I've gone from *I'll make amends* to *at least I didn't directly cause bodily injury like my best friend did.*

Regardless of everything, the bottom line is that she knows my secret and I know hers. She will accept me and help me despite what I did, and it's only fair that I do the same for her. Not only should I support her like she so obviously supports me, but what's the alternative?

If I tell the police she murdered Abby, not only will they likely find no supporting evidence, but I'll be in their crosshairs once again. Not to mention that if she were to discover I was the one who ratted her out, she could turn around and throw me under the bus.

I have to accept what we both did. I have to live with what we both did. I can either treat it like I'm upholding an obligation to a close friend, or I can act like she's holding something over my head. I find more comfort in knowing that we love and will both continue to protect each other and our secrets.

I must have fallen asleep eventually because I startle awake to discover rays of sun shining into the living room.

As I blink the sleep away from my eyes, everything from last night comes crashing back into focus.

I check the time and see that I was able to get a solid six hours of sleep, which is surprising, given the circumstances.

I observe an unread-text notification and tap it to see that Lucas has sent the message, but it's from hours ago. Likely a good-morning text. Yikes, it's almost eleven on a workday. He likely thinks I'm ignoring him.

Fear grabs hold of my chest, and my eyes widen as I consider what Lucas will think once he knows. We are at such a fragile stage in our relationship that I'd hate to risk it, but I also don't know if I can keep this matter to myself.

I'm not even totally convinced that I can live with this. For all I know, this mental struggle will break me, and I'll confess. I can see it happening.

No, I don't want to lose a lover and my friends. No, I don't want Bianca's sacrifice to be in vain. No, I don't want to be imprisoned when I didn't murder someone intentionally.

I know my soul, though, and I'm not sure I can go on living a normal life while keeping this experience in the back of my head. I don't know if I can hold a conversation with someone without thoughts of murder and lies intermingling.

If I tell Lucas, he might make the decision for me. Sure, he loved me years ago, and it feels like our relationship picked up right where it started, but there's no way of knowing. I've grown as a person with all the time between us, and maybe he has too. We haven't communicated much about the extent of our relationship or our future. He may not even be as invested in us as I am.

I've done enough sitting around sulking and wallowing in misery. I'm going to tell him. I must. I'll always have Bianca if he can't accept my truth. Hell, I hardly accept my truth, so how can I expect him to?

Oh well. My mind made up, I text him to come over when he

gets off from work. I roll off the couch and get to work cleaning myself up. I want to be excited when I get a text back from him saying that he can't wait, but instead I'm terrified.

Regardless, I try to bring forth happy thoughts and put on a playlist of songs that we created the last time we were together. I do all the things I'd normally do—brush my teeth, shower, exfoliate, shave, moisturize, find a sexy outfit, spray what is likely far too much perfume, and apply a small amount of makeup.

Luckily, I get lost in the routine, and when I'm finally finished, I eat something to sustain my body, not to satiate any hunger. My appetite may very well now be nonexistent. I'm so nervous, which isn't anything new, that I even go back and brush my teeth again.

I sit on the sofa and look at the clock to see that he should ideally be here within the hour. As I wait, I begin to rehearse my confession. I try to think back to last night and how I made my revelation to Bianca. That went smoothly enough, so maybe if I stick with the same script, he might be just as willing to accept it as she was.

I shake my head, even though there's no one here to see me do it. I can't presume he'll react the same way. My relationship with him is different in type and in the number of years we've known one another. Not to mention that he and Bianca have differing personalities, which will come into play.

I have to be prepared for the worst. I look down at my outfit and purse my lips. At least my mug shot will be sexy as hell, I think, as I run my palm over my skirt and pull down my red blouse to ensure I'm showing a reasonable amount of cleavage.

My legs begin to shake, and I get a knot in my stomach as I sit and wait. He's always made me feel like this, though; my nerves always spike when he is near. As if I've summoned him, there's a knock on the door.

I walk to the door slowly to greet him, pushing out my breath in an attempt to regulate my nervous system.

As the door opens, that smile of his almost makes me forget how worried I was to have him come over. I could drown in it, the way his eyes smile alongside his mouth. Man, I've got it bad.

He embraces me right there at the door, squeezing me so tightly, and it's exactly what I need right now. I analyze every second and take in every moment, memorizing everywhere his body meets mine. The smell of sandalwood invades my senses as his beard delicately grazes my flushed cheek.

I commit this hug to memory like it's the last one I'll ever get. It may very well be, and for that reason, I squeeze him back just as firmly, refusing to let go. I sense him loosening his grip around me, likely to release me from the hug, but when he detects that I'm not willing to do the same, he tightens his hold once more.

"I'm absolutely okay with staying in this position all night. I have no complaints. Ten out of ten," he whispers into my ear.

I chuckle into his shoulder.

No one can make me laugh like he can. No one embraces me like he does. No one can compare. Without even thinking, I pull away only slightly to kiss him on the lips. I almost break the kiss to ensure that actual sparks don't set my house on fire.

I pull my lips from his only to rest my head on his chest. It's then that he realizes something may be wrong. I can tell as he tenses beneath my grasp.

I inhale his scent one more time before pulling away. I grab hold of his hand and tug him toward the sofa so that we can sit.

Once he's seated comfortably, he leans toward me and gently pulls me near him, guiding me to sit on his lap. I don't resist and only nestle into him, ensuring I am as close to him as possible.

"No way you're sitting across the sofa from me when you look this gorgeous," he says, causing a blush to spread across my cheeks.

"Stop," I tell him, slapping his knee.

"Is everything okay?"

This question is the one I've been dreading. The question I don't want to answer but know I must.

Chapter 40

Lucas

Of course, I listen to everything Zoey tells me emphatically. I always did and I always will. I watch her as she recounts her memories from that day.

Sometimes I drift off, too busy analyzing her. I can't help it. I'm obsessed. The dimple on her right cheek that's hardly visible unless she smiles, which she definitely isn't doing now. The small beauty mark under her left eye. Her blond hair, tucked behind her ear so her long bangs don't fall in front of her eyes. The tears that gather in their corners, not yet fully falling, instead braced at the edge. Her fear is almost palpable, as I can feel her pulse accelerate while my hand rests on her wrist. I even notice that she takes long, deep, labored breaths for support as she tells me her story.

In a sense, I'm relieved. I've been worried about a few things. At one point, I was concerned she might be interested in another man, but I was able to rule that out quickly.

I was even more worried that she'd realized I'd been watching her. I'm glad these tears aren't because she's become aware of my deception, of my monster.

She's been too busy and too focused of late. This whole

time, she's been stuck in her head, but not for the reason I was worried about. I was convinced that she was on to me. I was afraid the thoughts swirling in her head were because she noticed my silent pursuit.

Had I been too obvious? Had she ever noticed me as I sat in my truck, watching her get to work and load coffees in her car? God knows I've watched her enough times that she could have spotted me at least once.

Maybe when I started to like her posts, she noticed the pattern I used? It was fun, like a clever game she didn't know she was a part of.

Although she never awoke while I watched her sleep, I wondered if she could sense me there and if that was what had her on edge? I always tried to sneak in during the early morning hours to ensure she'd be deep in sleep. I still have my key from all those years ago. Well, I gave her back the key I had, but not before making a copy of it.

When we started talking again, I thought for sure she would confront me and tell me to back off. I could tell that first night that she was hesitant, that she had fears. She wouldn't have liked how I would have handled everything if that were the case. Luckily for her and for me, she seemed willing to give our relationship another shot.

Even once we reconnected, I could tell something was off. I couldn't say what it was exactly. Surely if she knew that I was stalking her, she wouldn't entertain me, right? I truly couldn't determine if she knew that she was the one for whom my monster yearned to escape his prison.

After we broke up, I never stopped thinking about her. I've never truly gone away. No way was I ever willing to do anything that would take me away from her. I lied and told her I tried the boat thing, but I don't think I ever could. Not if it meant being away from her.

I've always been here. Watching her every chance I could, taking pictures of her to tide me over until the next time I could see her. I don't know how I get anything done.

I compartmentalize when it's time for work. I try to zone in and do what is expected of me, but even then, thoughts of her infiltrate my mind.

I think the reason that I was so worried about Zoey catching on is that I've slipped up in the past and been confronted before. I have some lingering recollections of that time in my life, but I try not to focus on what I did wrong. Instead, I've learned from that experience and gotten better at hiding my true intentions, better at keeping my obsession in the shadows.

I knew Zoey wanted me just as much as I longed for her. There were never any other men in her life, none that were ever too serious, anyway. I just knew that she couldn't get over me like I couldn't get over her.

I escalated things between us without her knowing. I couldn't resist. I eased my way into the house and I'd watch her sleep, hoping that she was dreaming of me. I even went overboard and put a little tracking app on her phone one night while she was asleep. Really, it was useless because she didn't go a whole lot of places, but it was nice to know where she was if I was ever curious.

I thought that would be enough, but her reintroduction into my personal space set a fire that quickly got out of control. I had to have her. I needed her almost as much as I needed water. It's euphoric to have her back in my arms.

I left those notes too. Looking back now, it was a stupid idea. I wanted to scare her in a way that would send her running back to me; but for a little while, it seemed like I was just planting seeds of doubt about me in her head, so I stopped leaving them.

I can't help but hate that Zoey feels like this. I hate that this has been on her chest all this time and she thought that she couldn't tell me. I want her to feel the same immense pleasure that I do. Maybe now that she's told me what's been bothering her, she can find solace and comfort in my presence.

I'm happy she feels like she can confess to me. Something like this is difficult to share with others. I would know. Hell, I never plan on telling her the things from my past. I know they're unacceptable; that's why I try so hard to prevent them. This will take our relationship to the next level. She'll know that she can trust me and that I won't betray what she has told me in confidence.

I accept her with all my heart, no matter what.

Chapter 41

Zoey, six months later

For a long time, I believed I wouldn't be able to live with what I did. The memories permeated my thoughts, and the guilt saturated my every waking moment.

I think what made it bearable was having Bianca and Lucas by my side. Their presence allowed me to push away the negative thoughts. Their kindness and support made me realize I didn't have to be defined by the one thing I did wrong.

A few times, I came close to turning myself in, but Lucas and Bianca were able to talk me off the ledge. I've finally gotten to the point where I'm comfortable with my decision.

It was an accident.

That has become my new mantra. I didn't mean for him to get hurt. I didn't hurt him intentionally. Luckily, I don't have to tell myself that too often. My thoughts run rampant in other areas now. I'm always fantasizing about my future with Lucas. The things we'll do, the places we'll go. Sometimes I imagine us married with children, or as grandparents retiring to the mountains.

I'm so busy being happy that I almost don't have time for negative thoughts. Even the sleepwalking has stopped, and it's so nice to feel rested and to not find things misplaced and moved around in my home.

I never thought I'd experience serenity again. I only hoped I could get back to my old self, but now it's even better; I'm better. I don't choose my relationship over my friends, and Lucas understands, although he misses me when I'm gone and tells me profusely.

He's actually begun slowly moving his things over to my house, so he won't get many more chances to miss me. I hang out with the girls often, holding true to my vow to reconnect and stay in touch with them. Bianca comes over all the time now too. It's like she knows I love her and that I also love Lucas, so she's taken it upon herself to ensure they can both have time with me. It's great that I don't have to choose between them.

Work's still an important part of my life as well. I was always blessed to have such a fun job and to be able to work with such kind people. It's still that way, and I love what I do.

The only thing different is that I don't stalk homes and enter without permission anymore. No, no, no. Never again.

I found a new outlet for my insatiable appetite for learning information about others. I often bid in online auctions for storage units that have been abandoned or are delinquent in their payments.

It's a lot like what I was doing, except it's legal! Actually, there are lots of great perks to it, and I can't believe I hadn't thought about it before.

I never know what I'll find when I bid, but that's part of the fun. I have it down to a science now. I bid on a local unit, trying not to spend too much money. Once I win the bid, I get so excited that I get to the unit as fast as possible, which is good because you actually are required to do that.

Ideally, I ask the owners if they have an available unit in their facility, and if so, I rent it, because after purchasing the contents, it's mandatory to remove them.

I try to savor the first official entrance into the storage unit to which I've just won all the contents. I open the door and look over my new belongings with pride, as if I'm a queen watching over her kingdom. I absorb it all. The dust particles that swarm into the air as the door rises. The musty smell of untouched items. The mysterious treasures that lie in unmarked boxes strewn about, sometimes orderly and sometimes haphazardly.

Just to hold me over, just to get a taste, I usually open one box while I'm there. I take my time when I go through it. I never go in with the intention of finding anything specific. No, I find pleasure in discovering facts that I didn't know before. Every unit is a lesson in what people deem important, or rather, unimportant, depending on how you look at it.

I pace myself, and it's refreshing that I can now that I don't have to worry about getting caught. The only thing I have to account for is the requirements set forth by the owner of the storage unit, since they usually want it emptied within seventy-two hours, but that's a whole lot more time than I used to get.

After I savor the moment of exploring one random box, it's time to get to work moving everything into another storage unit. That's the worst part, but luckily, Lucas helps me if it seems like too much. I move it all into my temporary unit, where I can begin to start my favorite part. Digging!

I never intend to keep anything, which is good because I couldn't afford to keep collecting and storing people's belongings. I really am just nosy. I want to see what they have. I want to pretend and imagine who they are.

I like to visualize the reasons they couldn't afford the rent, or speculate if they've since passed away and have no use for the items that remain.

Typically, I spend a month enjoying my discoveries, since I pay the rental-unit fee for a month, anyway. I go through everything from the unit at a leisurely pace, searching through totes and boxes to the crevices and drawers of furniture. I typically end up throwing many of the contents in the dumpster, especially since I can't hoard them all away.

I find things like old party decorations, board games, weights, and fishing or hunting gear. My primary focus isn't so much to make a dime, just to be nosy and dig through another person's belongings. I will say that some of the larger items, like furniture, I'll sell if they're in good condition. That way, the people who buy them can get rid of them so that I don't have to.

I'm a softy, so some things I can't bear to throw away, like family photo albums and sentimental keepsakes. In those cases, I keep the objects in the shed at my house just in case anyone ever comes looking or if I find their rightful home.

Occasionally, one of the girls will tag along to see if there's anything she may want to keep or to rummage and laugh with me about some of the things we find nestled away in boxes and crates. Lucas comes with me, too, sometimes, but more to be with me than to browse through strangers' possessions.

I simply dig and dig to my heart's desire until everything's thrown away or sold, and then it's time to start looking for another unit on which to bid.

For now, I'm happy with life, and it feels like I can forget the negatives in my past and start to concentrate on the future.

Things pop into my head here and there but not nearly as often as they once did. Like the notes. I haven't received any more of them, and while I'm glad, I'll never stop wondering where they came from.

The media focused on the theory that the first murder was a botched attempt by the Southern Slasher and that he rectified his mistake by murdering the second person. I should be in the clear, but you never really know. Cases get reopened, and new information tends to come to light with time. It's not typical, but it's also not unheard of.

Sometimes I wonder what the Southern Slasher thinks about it. I wonder if he's mad we brought attention to him, or if he's upset he was impersonated. Or is he... or she honored that there's a "copycat" out there that they think strives to rise to their standards? I hope I never find out.

Chapter 42

Lucas

I couldn't have asked for a better outcome with Zoey. We're back together again, and with time, her mental struggles have subsided, and she finally seems happy. These days, she is more like herself.

I hate to say this, but I appreciate that she was distracted when I first came back into the picture. That kept me in the clear. She never found out I was so obsessed with her that I was stalking her. Now she's just as obsessed with me as I am with her, so it all worked out.

Another thing she never found out was that she isn't the only one responsible for killing the man in the house.

I am too.

I knew her route and could track her with my phone, so occasionally I would pick up jobs that were near her so I could watch her. That day, I had just finished up a job and started driving around, looking for her car. I soon discovered her car abandoned, but finding it empty as I passed by confused me, since I didn't see her on the street either.

I pulled up to the intersection, took a right, and parked there to pull up the tracking app I had installed on her phone.

Sure enough, it showed that she was across the road from her car. I got out of my truck and walked toward the house.

I didn't even think because I didn't know what to think. Was she seeing someone I didn't know about? Why was she here? I had to know more, and so I stormed up to the house. It seemed quiet inside, and I didn't know what to do. I had my work gloves in my pockets, and as a last-minute thought, I pulled them out and slipped them on. I pulled on the front door slightly, but it didn't budge. I worked my way around the house and tried the side door, which was how I got in.

There was no other car at the house, which I thought was peculiar, too, but I told myself not everyone owned a vehicle. As I entered the house, I thought I heard shuffling from what I presumed was a bedroom.

Anger pulsed through me, even though Zoey and I weren't together. Technically, she wasn't betraying me by being with another man. I tried to remain calm as I inched slowly toward the open door. It was so risky to watch her that closely while she was so obviously awake, but I had to know what she was doing.

I watched her from the doorway, her back turned to me as she gently opened drawers and moved things around as if she were searching for something. I was so relieved that she was alone. Actually, the entire house appeared empty except for her.

I started going back the way I came, eager to escape before she found out I was there. I had more questions than answers, though, so I started to look around to try to determine why she was in that house.

I was in the kitchen, looking through pieces of mail, when I heard a noise that chilled me. The click of a door opening.

The sound came from the door that I entered from—the one in the laundry room that was right on the other side of the wall. Someone was coming inside.

I ducked down behind the counter, unsure of what to do. I'd never seen Zoey here before, but I tried not to watch her too much for fear of getting caught. Maybe this was her new boyfriend's house, and that was why she was here. Judging by the name on the mail I saw, he was the only occupant.

Not only could he not have Zoey, but I couldn't let him find me there. I didn't have to worry for long before Zoey came out and their confrontation ensued.

I watched his head hit the ground. Watched as the blood began to seep from the open gash in his skull. I sat there as he died, but he wasn't dying fast enough.

Zoey doesn't know that he was still alive after she fled. She will never know that I noticed he was still breathing. I couldn't let him survive in fear of him being able to identify her, so I smashed his head into the tile a few more times for good measure.

Hearing Zoey finally tell the story from her perspective cleared up a lot of things for me. She feels guilty because she thinks she killed him. I guess it's hard for me to understand, because I've killed in the past and I don't feel guilt.

Afterwards, I froze for a moment and took off my gloves to discover that my hand was shaking. I soon realized that Zoey might call the police, and I had to go before they arrived. I stood and tried to leave so fast that my free hand had grazed a cat figurine on the counter as I turned, and the force sent the miniature toppling over. It was stupid to have taken off the one thing protecting me from leaving my DNA at the scene. The object was just a decoration, though, and the dead guy wasn't going to miss it, so I swiped it and put it in my pocket to ensure I left nothing to indicate that I had been there.

I do feel bad she thinks it's her fault but not bad enough to tell her she's wrong. If I do, she'll want to know how I know, and that's not something I'm willing to share with her. With time, she's lightened up and gotten happier, which eases the bit of guilt I have for her carrying my burden.

I'm pleased she felt vulnerable enough to tell me her truth, because I'm sure not strong enough to confess mine to her.

After we broke up, I occupied myself; I had to so I could take my mind off her. My monster had a craving for another beautiful girl, Audrianna. She had the silkiest skin and always smelled like strawberries.

I really messed that one up. I had her in the palm of my hand until she realized the only reason that we had so much in common was because I followed her everywhere and memorized all her hobbies and interests. I'm sorry she's gone, but that's what happens when my monster overtakes me. I can't control how I'll react. I also can't take it back. The anger coursed through me that night—the night Audrianna told me I was demented and she could never love me.

She's gone now, and no one will ever know what I did to her. Luckily, our interaction was brief, and no one knew I was connected to her. She lived nearer New Orleans, where people go missing all the time. Ultimately, that's why I lock away the facet of me that is a vile and filthy creature.

I don't want to hurt anyone, but sometimes I can't help it.

I think that was one reason I was so worried Zoey would know I'd been watching her. I was found out once before.

My monster came out and took over the day I killed Alan. I was already angry, believing him to be important to Zoey.

Finding out he was a stranger didn't resolve the issue at hand, especially after she killed him. Even in death, he could have taken her away from me. He was dying, but just to be cautious, I had to make sure he was dead.

I was wrong, though. Kind of. Initially, I felt I was losing her to him. In a way, his coming home when he did would have made me lose her, but not in the way I thought at the time.

If I hadn't been there to guarantee his death before the police arrived, he could have identified her, and they would have arrested her and taken her away from me.

Zoey didn't realize how much she needed me in her life, but she does now.

Epilogue

Zoey

It's taken months, but I finally feel like things are all falling into place.

I look around my room and relish the new contributions from Lucas. He's adorned the walls with some emo band posters, which almost seems childish, but I love how he feels comfortable enough to be himself. This place is our home now. The first step toward our future.

I have the boxes of his clothes on my bed. They were resting in the corner, but with him putting some of his things away in the kitchen, I decided I could easily put away his clothes to help the process along. I tuck his shorts into one drawer, and I return to the bed to dig through the next box.

The cardboard scratches as I pry the flaps loose, and the sound is music to my ears. It's a sound that signifies the merging of two separate lives into one.

As I peer at the contents, I giggle to myself upon discovering my boyfriend's *consons*, as he likes to call them, instead of what they are in English, which is underwear.

I pick up the soft, worn fabric—and startle as my fingers hit something cold and heavy buried beneath it.

I push his underwear to the side to reveal the hidden object. My fingers tremble as I caress the familiar figurine. It's identical to the one I moved on the day that changed everything.

Why would Lucas have the opposing bookend from Alan's house?

A chill runs down my spine at the realization. This bookend is the exact same one, and I can tell because there's a small chip on the ear of the cat, which stands on its hind legs.

Why does Lucas have this?

I begin to shake as the implication of its presence becomes clear.

Logically, there is only one reason he'd have this figurine, and as hard as it is for me to understand, I still try.

He would have had to have taken it before the house became a crime scene. If he has it now, then he took it after I moved it and before the police found Alan's body.

That's an uncomfortably small time frame. It means Lucas was in the house with me.

He must have seen what I did.

But wait, why would he take this? It doesn't make sense.

I stare at the figurine as I hold it in my shaking hands. It's just as heavy as it was the day I first touched it.

Suddenly the truth begins to emerge as a clear picture appears in my mind.

Did Lucas kill Alan? But how, when I know I did? Why was Lucas there?

Oh my God.

Sweat beads down my forehead as thoughts fight one another for dominance.

It can't be. I remember it, or at least I thought I did.

I also thought I was being stalked. I thought I was innocent. I thought I could trust Lucas.

I think a lot of things, and I think way too much.

It's him. It's always been him.

He's never said anything.

I hear shuffling from behind me, and I turn around to meet Lucas's eyes. He comes to a halt upon seeing my face, and his glance soon sweeps down to the figurine I'm holding.

His eyes quickly dart back up to mine, and I see fear flash across his face.

Is it fear that I'll turn him in for the murder? Fear that he'll lose me?

Neither of us speaks. I don't want to sway his admission, and he likely doesn't know what I'm thinking, afraid to speak and place ideas in my head.

"Why?" I ask, a quiver in my voice as I hold back tears.

I don't even know what I'm asking.

Why kill him?

Why haven't you told me?

Why were you there?

"For you. Everything I do is for you."

My heart cracks—figuratively, of course, but I can almost feel it in my chest.

I'm sane, or at least I like to believe I am, although I know I have quirky and unusual habits. I know how I should feel: afraid, betrayed, alarmed.

I feel none of those things. Instead, I'm honored he has helped keep my secret.

He did it for me. He knows me better than most people do, and he's still here. I have no doubt that he has done and will do anything to keep me safe, although we need to have a talk about secrets and lies of omission.

I walk slowly toward him and hold the figurine to his chest as I hover inches away.

"A symbol of our commitment?" I ask him, slowly bringing my eyes up to meet his.

The tension falls from him. I see his shoulders slacken and feel his chest fall as he exhales in relief.

"It's us against the world, Rosy," he says, wrapping his arms around me, the heavy bookend poking me as he squeezes me closer to him.

I soften beneath his touch, leaning my head against his shoulder.

I've been so fulfilled these last few months. I've begun to make plans for my future, all of which include Lucas.

If we can get through this... I imagine we can get through anything.

This is one scenario I could never have dreamt up, but that just makes it even more special.

Acknowledgments

I am so thankful for many people in my life who have supported me, encouraged me, and inspired me! I may not name every single one of you, but know as you read this book that you were on my mind and it is what it is because of all of you! Writers tend to write what they know, so if there was something in here that sounded familiar, it was likely inspired by you!

Thanks to my dad for being the first beta reader to return the book with edits to prove that he read it (and fast too)! Thanks to my mom, because she brings my book with her to all her doctor's appointments and brags about me endlessly.

Thanks to Jasmine for being so supportive while I write and when it comes to telling people about my books! That goes for Connie too, who is basically my agent with all the promotions she does for me without me having to ask! To Stephanie, you came in clutch for me once I got some feedback from my editor who suggested an alternate ending. Thanks for helping me decide what to do!I'm thankful for all my coworkers and their support.

Many thanks to my beta readers for their feedback and the donation of their time to help me publish my second thriller book!

Thanks to Teresa and Devin who so graciously offered their personal time to cheer me on and help me brainstorm titles for this book. I am thankful for my husband, John, for his honest feedback and willingness to read my book when he hasn't read any since high school. I am thankful for my daughter who inspires me and brings the sunshine into my life. Thanks to my godchildren and nephew; Zeke, Allison, and Jameson (who will read this and hopefully be so excited that their names are in a book) for loving your nanny and tante.

Thank you to Dr. Camille Pitre for her help with Cajun French terminology. Big thanks and so much love goes out to Papa Callais who is in heaven and is surely one of my biggest fans! I'm so thankful for all my friends and followers as without their insistence I may have not written another book.

Thanks to each and every individual who asked me about this book, commented on my indecisive posts, cheered me on through the process, and may have inspired certain characters...thanks!

If you guys didn't like the names, don't blame me. My friends made me do it.

Speaking of...I am very thankful for some of my greatest and purest friends; Mikki, April, Kim, and Nikki. Bianca's character was a combination of you 4, and I won't say which one of you I think is capable of murder. Okay, okay, a hint: you have an I in your name.

Karla, so happy you went from a local reader to a prized and cherished ARC reader!

If I didn't say your name specifically, forgive me! This book was so fun to write, but I've been trying so very hard to publish it before the end of 2025 as a goal for myself. That being said, it has me a little scatterbrained as I comb over it repeatedly to ensure it's the best book for my readers! I am thankful for each and everyone of you guys!

About the Author

Heather Chauvin has always enjoyed writing and story-telling, and loves the challenge of predicting plot twists in both books and movies. She currently holds a Bachelor's degree in Communication Disorders and a Master's degree in Science. Heather is a full time Speech-Language Pathologist, working with individuals age 0-100 years old. She is passionate about facilitating communication for both children and adults in southern Louisiana. She also enjoys reading, board games, and spending time with her beautiful family among other things. Of all her accomplishments, her ability to lick her elbow reigns supreme. Heather often enjoys spiraling into hypothetical situations in her head, as well as with friends. Find her on Facebook!

Also by Heather S. Chauvin

Camp Sunshine: A Thrilling Domestic Novella
Three couples. Two kids. One camping trip gone horribly wrong.

Lion City Adventure
Written with her daughter, this children's story is about some kids that go on a little adventure.

Horror for the Holidays
A group of independent authors came together to each write a chapter for a thrilling Christmas tale!